The Rewilding:
A Tale From The Weald

.

H.R MacDonald

Disclaimer and Copyright

The author is in no way responsible for the actions of the reader. This is a work of fiction. Any and all names, places, events and incidents here within are used in a fictitious manner. Any resemblance to actual persons living or dead, or actual events is purely coincidental.

Table Of Contents

Wealdenperspective.wordpress.com

"When the last tree is cut, the last fish is caught, and the last river is polluted; when to breathe the air is sickening, you will realize, too late, that wealth is not in bank accounts and that you can't eat money." - Alanis Obomsawin

Prologue

An unrecognisable landscape from five years before stretched out for countless miles across the formerly overpopulated countryside.

The frigid winter mist drifted over the silent and still hills which were covered in every kind of herbaceous plant, from deciduous ancient Oaks and coniferous Yews to the smallest sapling of Ash and Hornbeam. Underneath the heavy canopy of bare branches, which had been whitened with a fresh layer of snow, the old frayed track made its way through the valley. Only a small amount of sunlight filtered through the canopy and down onto the frozen ground, the sun setting quickly at the shortest time of the year. The tiny tracks of deer making their way across the road, quickly fading from the new snow falling from the branches above.

The sound of footsteps made their way from the distance. Alerting all the animals in the vicinity. A crow taking to flight, squawking as it did so, created a sharp piercing noise in the calm silence.

Around the narrow bend at the neck of the road came three men, wrapped up in thick furs and other old world garments which they had scavenged. They walked in a line quietly and quickly, however not too fast, as sweating in such cold weather would be a fatal mistake if it froze to the body.

They chose their path wisely, trying to make as little noise as possible and it was effective with the snow muffling much of the noise caused by their footsteps.

"Have any of you got the feeling that we are being watched?" asked one of the men, his voice difficult to hear with the warm woollen scarf wrapped around his neck and his head covered by a thick hood.

"Stop being so paranoid Thorburn, if we have to stop every five minutes because of you then we'll never get to the Fortress" said the man at the front of the line, he was dressed in very much the same way but carried a large flag which was on a pole hanging over his shoulder. The image bedecked on it was that of the ancient Sol rune black in colour, pointed at both ends on a red background and underneath a smaller crescent moon, white in colour.

"I know Ron, but I just have bad feeling. What do you think Alex?" said Thorburn, his anxiousness was plain to see.

"I think we should keep going and be quiet, If something is following us then it will make itself known eventually" said Alex, he was older than the other two men and thought of himself as the leader of the group, it was he who carried the important documents relating to the quarterly report from The Trundle. Its

contents included reports of births/deaths, food/water quantity and situation, crop quality and harvest reports, livestock numbers and sightings of the Archons.
The olive coloured satchel bag on his side carried these important and highly valued documents.

They continued walking but at a slightly slower pace. The track began to go upwards in a slight incline and to the sides the undergrowth had grown thickly obscuring their view further up the track.
They had to stop in order to cut a small path through the blockage. Thorburn unsheathing his old and trusty machete for the job and beginning to hack away at the frozen branches in front of him.
At the back Ron leaned lazily on the standard he held in his hand, yawning to himself. It was in this daze of laxness that he caught movement out of the corner of

his eye.

A shape, close to ground creeping its way behind them expertly. Not making a sound as it made its way towards them. Stopping when it knew it had be seen for only a fraction of a second. Waiting to make its next move.

"Guys, something just moved in the woods next to the track" said Ron, who was now facing the way they had just come from and scanning the trees for further movement.

"Not you as well, there is nothing in the trees. You're spooking yourselves" replied Alex, trying to sound rational. Thorburn stopped chopping and turned around as well, they all stood in silence for a minute and all that could be heard was the relaxing noise of the wind blowing through the trees and the silence of the falling snow above them. Ron turned back around and before he could say his next sentence a white flash burst from the undergrowth. Landing on top of him like a rod of lightning from the sky.

It took Thorburn's brain a second to comprehend what he was seeing In front of him. Ron's body was limp and covered in blood as a huge Tiger, white in colour and effectively camouflaged to the winter surroundings stood over him with its jaw clamped down on his neck, shaking the last particles of life from him. The pole with the standard had flown out of his hand and landed at Thorburn's feet. He picked it up, not being able to take his eyes of what he was seeing. Alex was in a sort of trance as well, staring with wide eyes at what was in front of him.

The Tiger, once it knew that Ron was no longer living dropped his body to the ground and looked up at his next victim. Alex tried to slowly work his way backwards, never taking his gaze away from the golden eyes of the predator in front of him. Thorburn was stuck to the spot, frozen like the cold ground beneath his feet.

The Tiger had no interest in him however and was fixated on his friend who had backed himself up against the fallen branches. It was within a second that his flight or fight response finally kicked in and he made a dash for it. Running as quick as he could he scrambled under the blockage and down the road but Thorburn was behind him, the tiger in-between them. In his haste to escape Alex lifted the satchel which carried the important documents and threw it over his head, straight into the path of Thorburn who was taken by surprise as it hit him in the chest and he caught it like it was an oversized rugby ball. The ghost like tiger wasn't fazed by the large bag flying over its head and continued chasing Alex, getting closer and closer with each stride before it was on top of him. The screams filled the void of silence which encompassed the forest and it began to fade as Thorburn ran further and further down the winding track, hoping with every fibre of his being that when he next looked over his shoulder the unfamiliar feline shape was not following him as he knew he wouldn't be able to outrun it.

After a few seconds the screams stopped as the large canine teeth sunk into the windpipe of the middling aged man, ending his earthly existence. The feline had no interest in the third human who was now running for his life down the snow covered track. He had enough meat to keep him going for a few more weeks. His head swung from side to side and he sniffed the air for anything that might threaten to take his human dinner. He then grabbed the limp human, who in his jaw felt like a small rag doll, and began to drag him back to his lair high in the chalky hills which overlooked the road. For the graceful tiger it was just another day of survival in the natural world in which he lived. A great comparison to the rest of his life in which he was trapped living in a concrete and steel cage. He felt free.

Thorburn kept running, his lungs burning like hot coal but the adrenaline flowed and numbed the pain. He didn't dare look over his shoulder out of fear of seeing the white mass following behind him. It was only when the adrenaline stopped pumping that he began to slow, the pain being too much for him to continue. He looked behind him precariously, trying to see the Tiger but everything had gone back to that quiet, pristine sound of nature.
His objective was not far now, being just below the Downs. He could see the roofs and small clouds of smoke coming from chimney stacks floating up into the sky.

His pace picked up at seeing such a sight and he began to jog the last few hundred metres.

The gate was getting closer and he held the standard up high, allowing the slight breeze to catch it.
"It's Thorburn, open up quick!" he shouted to the sentry's standing idly on the stained wooden palisade.
The gate began to swing open, Thorburn lent on the standard but it wasn't enough to keep him up and he crumpled into a pile on the dirty track.
Exhaustion had got the better of him.

<u>Chapter I</u>

The snow and frost shined in the late
morning sun which cast its warming
light over the land. Down below the
magnificent humpbacked Downs sat the
main settlement of the hill people. It was
an ancient village before the collapse of
the old world and that ancient style still
resonated through the architecture of
most of the buildings. Thatched roofs
and flint walls abounded in that beautiful
Sussex style and the former road snaked
its way through the centre of the village,
passing the Church with its large copper
spire, although it was long since any
religious matter took place within its
walls and it was now used as a
watchtower, and continued through the
main street. The streets were clean and
well kept and the buildings much the
same. On most of the buildings hung
boughs of Holly, their prickly waxen
leaves moving slightly in the breeze. It

was customary at this time of year to hang Holly on doors and window sills going back to the ancient traditions of thousands of years before where it was said that Holly warded off evil spirits. Unlit lanterns also decorated most the flint buildings which had smoke wafting from their chimneys. Warming them due to the freezing temperatures.

People were busy rushing around, greeting each other in the street. Children played in the snow and snowballs flew through the air like missiles. Many of the children didn't remember the time before the collapse and the warm winters which had occurred preceding that great change which had happened five years before. They only knew cold, snow graced winters and warm, wet summers.

The small, crystal clear stream ran underneath the main road and fed the rest of the surrounding land, giving it life.

Much of the land which before had been left fallow or been wasteland in the hands of landlords who only wanted to increase their profits was now turned into fertile growing space for vast amounts of produce. The inhabitants had created an extremely effective and environmental system that in the old-world was called 'Permaculture'. Each of the few hundred inhabitants did their part and helped cultivate and harvest the food which fed them all. As well as the growing plots, which were empty due to the time of the year, their were a few dozen greenhouses which had been found and assembled nearby. Allowing them to grow some more exotic produce such as tomatoes and chillis.

At the centre of the village, which to the people living there and in the surrounding area was colloquially called 'The Fortress', was the large school building, and village hall. The school building was that of the rough, Brutalist type and was now a lot smaller as some of the rooms were used for storage while the rest were used for the schooling of the settlements younger inhabitants. The Village hall on the other hand was built in a more aesthetically pleasing style and was well kept even after the collapse. Outside of the hall a large group of people were moving tables and chairs, hanging decorations from the building and trying to build a large temporary gazebo next to the hall.

Helping lift some boughs of Holly up to the men standing on the ladders was Rebecca. On her chest in a well-made baby sling was her newborn daughter Elfin, snuggled in the sling warm and fast asleep, and crawling around close next to her was her other young daughter Rose, who looked like a young bear due to her fur clothing and hat. She was looking at the ground intensely, trying to find bugs and other insects in the soil.

Rebecca finished helping with the decorations and began to walk around the area inspecting how things were going. The fires were being made for the feast later in the day and the tables were being put into place quickly. Walking inside and the change in temperature was almost uncomfortable, with the heat hitting her.

A woman was moving boxes of produce such as potatoes, carrots, onions, apples, pears, plums and berries into the small backroom. She was young, short in stature wearing a long colourful dress and apron, and also had her hair covered with a piece of old fabric.

"Good morning Ms. Baker, how are things going?" said Rebecca, walking over and helping lift some of the boxes.

"They are going quite well I must say, we are only waiting on the meat to be delivered now, Angus said he'll be here by noon with the pork and chicken" Her voice rang with the Sussex dialect which most of the people who lived in the Settlements had.

"Earl and my brother have just arrived so you should have some more food coming by shortly. They have gone to see Cyril first and their people are being shown to their accommodation" replied Rebecca, moving the sling and checking Elfin who was cuddled up next to her mother. She smiled slightly as she looked down as she always did.

Rose who was just behind Rebecca tried to crawl into the small room but her mother stopped her.

"Hello Rose" said Ms. Baker, her face lighting up as she watched the young girl crawling around. "I have a treat for you". She rooted around in one of the boxes and pulled out a punnet of blackberries which had been saved from the late autumn. She gave Rose a few of them which were quickly eaten.

"She is growing fast isn't she" said Ms.-

Baker

"Indeed she is, not as quick as her brothers though".

They spoke for a few more minutes before Rebecca decided to go and find Cyril, Earl and her brother. Walking back out into the bright winter sun and frigid air she made her way to the large house which was situated across the empty plots of growing land and greenhouses. The house was in a prominent spot amongst the leafless trees. Its former gardens being turned into another plot for the production of edible produce. It was built in Sussex flint and was in that beautiful Victorian Gothic design with equally spaced bay windows, decorative fascia and cornice and bright red roof tiles which were replaced very soon before the collapse occurred.

She walked through the garden and opened the glass back door which led into the large and airy living room. Elfin began to stir in her bundle and Rose was being carried and taking great interest in what her little sister was doing.

In the living room a group of men were sat on the sofas and chairs, talking amongst themselves before standing as Rebecca made her way through the door. "Good morning gentlemen, I hope you had a good journey" she said.
"Indeed we did. The journey was arduous but we made it" replied a young man, wearing a mail shirt over a large gambeson, a long Seax at his side. His face covered by a large blonde beard and his hair which was cropped close to his head being the same colour. The other men in the room nodded in agreement. They were all Earls' Thegns. Men of great martial skill and loyalty. They all wore similar attire of mail shirts and carried the customary Seax on their belt. Their shields and spears were resting against the wall across the room, always in arms reach.

"Is my husband in his study with Earl and my brother?" she asked

"Indeed they are"

"Thank you gentlemen, help yourself to refreshments in the kitchen and make yourself at home."

They all stood as she left the room making her way through the house to the small study room which was at the back end of the building. She could hear her brothers voice as she got closer.

The door was open wide and she knocked on it jokingly which made all of the men In the small room turn around at the same time.

The small room had three windows which allowed in the bright morning sunlight. In between the windows were large bookcases which were filled with all kinds of books, from fiction to non-fiction and also a large collection of Tabletop Role-Playing Game manuals. They were her and Cyril's personal collection of books. In the village she had also started to create a public library for everyone. Books were highly valued in the New World in which they lived.

In the middle of the room was a large oak desk, covered in maps and other documents. Cyril was sat at the head of the desk. He was wearing his mail shirt much like the rest of the men in the room. His beard was long since he began growing it earlier in the year, it was brown in colour but flecked with blonde. He stood up when he saw her.

Around the desk were her brother who stood proudly and next to him Earl, while the others were the Thegns of all three of the leaders. Even in a room with over a dozen men Earl still towered over them.

"Good morning everyone. You look busy" she said with a smile on her face.

It brought a smile to the group in the room as well and some repressed laughs.

"We are looking at sending an expedition to the coast if you are planning on volunteering" said Anderson, knowing he was the only person in the room who could get away with saying such a jest. "Like always you send me to do the job for you little brother, nothing ever changes."

Her comment made many in the room laugh aloud, not being able to hold in the repressed laughter. Anderson turned bright red, embarrassed at being made a fool.

"Nice to see you again Earl, it's been a while. How's Emily and the children?"

"They are very well Rebecca, thank you for asking. They are with the others being shown accommodation and should be around soon." His gruff Sussex accent reverberated around the room.

"Good, I'm happy to hear it" she replied.

"So what are the plans for this expedition?" she asked Cyril, rocking Elfin in her arms as she spoke.

"We are planning to send a few men

down to the coast to check the water quality and see if it is viable for fishing. But we have had reports from Earl that the water is covered in oil slicks and could be contaminated with nuclear waste" he said, taking a pause. "But the problem is we cannot agree if it is safe to send an expedition or not at the moment. Especially after what happened to Thorburn, Alex and Ron a few days ago"

"I think we should wait until after the Jul celebration before we do anything. We can send a group after that" said Earl after Cyril had finished.

"A good idea. We should celebrate for the coming new year before we do anything else. It has been a hard few months" Cyril adjusted his papers on the table and stood up.

"What do you say Anderson?"

"I agree with you, let us have a few days of celebration, everyone deserves it"

"Well that settles it then. Enjoy the celebrations, Health and happiness to you all" said Cyril, at which their were reciprocal shouts of "Health and Happiness" from the group of men in the room.

They began to filter out as Rebecca stepped into the quickly emptying room, standing next to her brother and facing Cyril.

"You shouldn't be doing any work today my love, It is the solstice, you should be having fun and celebrating" she said to Cyril as he collected up the maps before putting them back into the bookcase behind him.

"I know, I know." he replied, "It's a fine day for it."

They left the room and the building, walking back towards the hall to oversee proceedings. Many people stopped to greet them as they walked. Cyril carried Rose in his arms, not bothered that a bit of dirt got on his mail shirt.

They took a detour before going to the

hall, a small field next the stream was filled with people all practising with mêlée weapons. Many a Seax was being swung, blunt to not cause injury. Spear shafts prodded at shields, wooden hafts simulating clubs and other blunt instruments crashed down on mail. Most of those taking part were young boys and teenagers. Mock shield-walls marched against each other with much laughter and some cries as a misplaced weapon hit a knuckle or elbow causing a second or two long bout of pain.

Cyril and the others stood watching, at the side of the field a small group were learning the techniques of swordsmanship. Their teacher being Björn, older than most in the settlement he was a master swordsman before the collapse, learning the skill as a hobby he never thought he would have to use. His grey hair was long and so was his beard which swayed as he swung the wooden sword through the air showing the youngsters the correct procedure.

Cyril smiled as his sons stood in the group, fumbling with each swing of the wooden swords and being generally clumsy like all novices are. His oldest son, Lyndon, stood at the front with the other similarly aged boys. All of them being born just after the collapse occurred five years before. And behind them was Renfred who was only three years old and was having trouble even lifting the wooden training sword let alone swinging it. He was watching his older brother, attempting to copy every manoeuvre.

Björn noticed Cyril and the others standing and watching, the large smile on Cyril's face plain to see.

They finished the last set of manoeuvres before Björn called a short break. The two brothers saw their parents and uncle and immediately ran over to them. Björn following close behind, his hands behind his back and his posture stooped over slightly like an old, wise eagle.

"Hello Dad" said Lyndon, full of excitement, "Did you see me swinging the sword?."

"Of course I did son, I'm very proud of you."

Cyril ruffled Lyndon's hair before speaking to Björn.

"How Is he getting along?"

The old wizened armourer took a few moments before answering.

"He is doing very well indeed, especially in speed and blocking manoeuvrers. If he continues improving at this rate I will have to move him up to the next grade early" his voice was like that of an old wizard and kept everyone captivated.

"His brother is also doing well for his age, I believe it is because he is copying his brothers techniques somewhat."

"Very good Björn, I'm happy to hear how he is improving. Will you be at the celebration tonight?"

"Of course I will" he chuckled, "When do I miss the opportunity for a jug of ale and a nice shank of meat."

"I look forward to seeing you there my friend, I will speak to you tonight" said Cyril before shaking his hand and allowing him to continue with his work, the break short but enough for the boys to catch their breath.

They began again on their walk towards the centre of the village and where the main celebrations would take place later in the evening. The ruralness of the settlement was everywhere with the hills rising up in the distance and rolling away to the horizon like chalk waves. In a small piece of land a large bonfire was being made, extra wood which had collected from abandoned places in the surrounding area at the side for use much later in the night. A man holding an acoustic guitar which had been kept in immaculate condition passed them on his way to the village hall, he would be supplying music for the inhabitants. Once they arrived at the village hall the decorations and tables were all ready and people were sitting around relaxing in the mid morning sun. Cyril inspected the area feeling satisfied. He decided to take a walk and see Thorburn who was recuperating in the village infirmary. It was an old semi-detached house which had originally been constructed by a family of farmers two centuries before. The wooden beams and whitewashed stone gave it an otherworldly look. In the windows could be seen some of the herbs used as medicine, while the rest of the building was stocked with a large selection of herbs and other medicinal plants which had been foraged, it was inhabited by an older woman who had been a nurse for many years in the old world.

He began walking on his own. It reminded him off the old days when he would go for walks in the countryside to clear his mind. Remembering when he first met Robert on that fateful summer day five years in the past, it seemed like a lifetime ago to him.

He walked through the pleasant lanes which glinted with frost in the morning light and was quickly at the makeshift infirmary. He walked up the short, slippery steps to the front door which was painted a deep burgundy and knocked a few times.

After a few seconds the door creaked open and a small, elderly woman stood in the doorway.

"Good morning young man, how can I help you?" she said.

"Good morning Mrs. Rake, I have just popped round to see if it is possible to speak to Thorburn about his trouble on the road the other day. I shouldn't be too long" he replied politely.

"Of course, please come in and wipe your feet. Would you like a drink?, I have the kettle on the fire."

"No thank you Mrs Rake, I won't have enough time unfortunately."

He stepped into the small house which was filled with all kinds of bric-à-brac which sat on most of the surfaces. The air was humid and stifling in the house due to the large wood burning stove which was blasting out heat in the sitting room. On the sofa under a pile of thick blankets was Thorburn, his face red and sweaty from fever. He had a hot cup of liquid next to him which had herbs floating around in it and also a pile of books to keep him occupied.

As Cyril walked into the room Thorburn sat up and turned himself towards Cyril.

"Hello Cyril" he croaked.

"Hello Thorburn, how are you feeling?"

"Not to bad actually, I feel as if I've finally started to warm up after these past few days. And I got some sleep but only a few hours"

"Good, you are safe now so you have

nothing to fear. I've come to see you to ask you about what you saw a few days ago. If you don't want to talk about it then please don't feel you have to." He pulled up a chair next to Thorburn and sat down, the sound of Mrs Rake humming from the kitchen filled the vacuum of silence when he stopped speaking.

A flash of fear ran through Thorburn's face as he remembered the experience of a few days prior. Staring into space before snapping himself out of it and looking back at Cyril.

"I don't know where to start. We left the Trundle and it was fine like always. The road was empty and all we saw and heard were the birds squawking in the trees and the occasional deer call. We also only saw fresh deer and boar tracks as we walked so nothing was out of the ordinary. Once we got into the woods just outside Chilgrove I started getting the feeling that I was being watched. I kept on telling the others but they just ignored me or laughed it off as paranoia. We continued on before we were stopped by a tree that was blocking the road. Being the man with the machete I began to hack at the branches to clear a way before Ron said... said he saw something move in the woods" he stopped, his stare going straight through Cyril before speaking again.

"Then this flash came out of the trees, it was white and I think it was nearly ten feet long from head to tail. It was a tiger... A white tiger." He began sweating profusely as the memory flashed in his mind again.

"It landed on Ron and began ripping at his neck, I think he must have died instantly with such a weight pressed on him, at least I hope he went quickly. I can't remember much after that, I was stuck to the spot frozen before I just started running. It was chasing Alex who was in front of me and he must have

thrown his bag off because it hit me in the chest and I caught it. I was lucky because the tiger was chasing him and had no interest in me. I ran past them both staring straight ahead and then I could hear him screaming in pain" tears began to form in his eyes which Cyril saw, he patted Thorburn on the shoulder to try and comfort him.
"Why would their be a tiger in the woods of Sussex, I just don't understand it Cyril" he sobbed.

Cyril cupped his chin in his hand while thinking,
"I have a theory as to why. It's the same reason we have wolves, bears, lynx and bison roaming freely. As the collapse occurred the zoo keepers opened the cages at the zoos and released all the animals. Quite a natural reaction as they didn't want the animals they cared for to die of starvation or thirst stuck in a cold cage. Many of these released animals

would have died of exposure due to not being adapted to the climate but some would have survived, especially those species which were on this island in the past before being made extinct. Their is a plentiful supply of prey like deer for them to eat."

Thorburn let what Cyril had just said roll through his mind before nodding slowly.

"Come to the festivities tonight if you feel well enough. It will take your mind off things" said Cyril before standing up and patting him on the shoulder again.

"I will if I can, I promise you that"

"Good, Health and happiness to you Thorburn" said Cyril.

"Health and happiness" responded Thorburn.

He thanked Mrs. Rake for her time and told her that he will bring Rebecca and the children to see her soon, she always enjoyed that.

He stepped back out into the cold and

carefully stepped down the slippery brickwork stairs wondering how many different wild predators were lurking In the area and how to take precautions to avoid them.

▲ ▲ ▲

Darkness had begun to fall quickly due to the day being the shortest of the year. The bonfire had been lit and its flames darted into the sky, shimmering with light and heat as it rose into the dark starlit sky. Groups of young adults ran around collecting the large bits of wood and launching it onto the bonfire, sending sparks up into the sky, shouts and laughter abounded. The village hall was filled with people, eating, drinking, singing and being merry after a long year of work. Some fires burned in the former carpark which was now turned into the outside seated area and meat was being grilled on them to feed the large group who had arrived. Fruit and other produce was on the tables and the ale flowed freely. Nobody drank too much, however, temperance was respected. Cyril sat at his own table with Rebecca and their family, Anderson and his wife, Freya who was heavily pregnant with there first child, sat next to them. Earl and his family also sat at the table. His wife named Emily and their three children named Oswald, Alfred and Erika.

They chatted and ate before Cyril stood up. The background chatter became silent with the only sound being that of the sizzling food and bonfire crackling in the distance.

He cleared his throat before speaking to the gathered crowd.

"I would like to thank everyone for coming to this celebration tonight, it has been a long year and we all deserve a rest and time to celebrate our achievements, especially over the last five years. We are free now and will be for the rest of time. The collapse led to a lot of sadness, suffering and strife for us all but we have overcome that and live in happiness in our tribe. Death is a constant companion in this world but we know that when we all finally pass we will live on in our children and their descendants for eternity. We have seen how nature has returned after being abused for so long and has reclaimed what is rightly hers. The cities crumble and fall to ruins. We have left our old lives behind, many of you have changed your names as a symbol of the New Age that we now live in and some haven't. Life is simpler and a struggle but we love it and wouldn't have it any other way. Thank you" he finished speaking and raised his mug before taking a sip. Cheers rang out from all those gathered before the merriment and feasting began again in full swing. It would be a long night.

Chapter II

A sea of tents and other ramshackle structures, wagons, carriages, wheel-barrows and two-wheeled trailers spread into the distance of a once great and peaceful woodland. All the trees had since been felled and most of them burnt. The river Wey which ran next to the ghetto like camp ground was filled with all kinds of rubbish and other detritus, which was caught in the reeds and other waterborne plants which swished slightly in the gentle current. Animals from domesticated dogs, cats and the livestock which were kept in disgusting conditions in the camp, waited nervously and in fear for their impending slaughter In the mud from their uninterested owners.

A group of chained people numbering fifteen individuals, young and old, male and female were being marched through the camp to the distaste of the unclean and uncouth inhabitants who shouted obscenities at them and tried to make them fearful. "Disgusting Yokels" shouted one woman with a toothless grin as she was leaning out of her tent, another spat at the group as they walked.

The children In the middle of the group were crying, their parents trying to shield them the best they could although each time they tried the men walking beside them holding the chains which bound them, pulled them away forcefully which led to cries of pain as the cold iron pinched their exposed skin. They were walking towards the centre of the tent city which was more cleared than the rest of the area, a square of sorts, although instead of being a clean orderly area free from obstructions it was filled with sloppy and gawm-like mud which stuck to their bare or clothed feet. Most of them shivered as they were only in thin clothes or pyjama-like attire which gave no protection from the freezing cold wind which blew down from the arctic north. A small hint of snowfall falling but melting instantly as it landed onto the wet mud.

In the centre of the ramshackle square was a huge tent. Bigger than any other in the tent city and around it was flying all kinds of different multicoloured flags which were bright in comparison to the brown, stained tent canvas. The group stood for minutes in silence. One of the individuals in the chained group coughed and was whipped with a long, thin branch for making a noise. The cracking sound made them all jump in fright. As they stood a crowd began to gather around them but not in front, where the entrance to the main tent was situated, instead they stood behind and around the group, waiting for their leader to reveal himself.

The slurs were still being thrown against them as they stood in silence with their chains rattling slightly from their constant shivering, many of them covered in mud themselves, their hair and clothes being turned brown and matted from it.

The door of the tent was then thrown open and four armed men marched out. Their faces covered in balaclavas which only had eye slits and were all black in colour. Their other clothing was the same colour and was stained with dirt and blood, looking like they hadn't been washed since before the collapse. They stood in a guarding position in front of the tent as the next person walked out. He was of average height and build with a shaved head. His face half between a smirk and manic laughter, his white vest being stained with so many different shades of red it looked like an artists palette. His arms covered in picked scabs from drug use. His face was scarred and disfigured from years of constant fighting. Two beady, almost black coloured eyes peered out of his stubbled face. He stood for a few moments with his hands on his hips, before letting out a tremendous laugh. Many of the people gathered in the crowd had already kneeled to their strange leader but some still stood.

"A new batch of slaves, how nice. But first they must learn how to become disciplined in my horde. Put them down on their knees" he shouted in such a tone that it made his voice crack, he did not know how to speak quietly.

They were all forced to kneel, some doing it of their own volition while others had the backs of their legs kicked viciously to force them down.
The leader of the horde then marched his way through the squelching mud towards them. His guards quickly

following him like lap dogs with their master.

"My name is Vesh and I am your master now. You will obey or you will die... or maybe worse. I know you Yokels think you are free in this horrible muddy swamp you call home but you aren't free."
He paced in front of them, stopping in front of one of the older males in the group, grabbing his head and kneeing him in the face in a second of rage. It sent a fountain of blood spurting out of the man's broken nose. He then began stamping on the injured man's body and head, making him writhe in agony which forced the thick mud to cover all over him as he struggled to protect himself.
"You all look to different, where is the trimmer?, bring me the trimmer!" At this command a man came out of the crowd holding a pair of large scissors. He awkwardly darted to Vesh before

bowing.

"Give them all the same trim. They don't need hair to work"

It took a few minutes for all of them to be shaved. What little warmth their hair gave them now gone as they shivered in the mud. They tried not to sob or make any noise out of fear of death or being beaten.

"Good, now you will be given your first assignment. You will have to survive the first night in our horde sleeping here in your chains. If you survive then we will except you, if you die then your friends can consume you because they will be hungry." Laughter rained from all around, much of it being genuine laughter while others laughed nervously, trying not to be seen to displease their leader.

He then clicked his fingers before going back into his warm tent and closing the canvas door.

The poor people in the mud sat in shock, huddling closer together to try and keep each other warm and thought about what Vesh had just said. The sound of the injured man, breathing deeply through his busted nose kept them awake but after a while the noise stopped as his life expired.

The camp went back to how it was before almost as if nothing had happened, with the haggled people crawling around in the mud and being generally disgusting in their ways.

▲ ▲ ▲

Although the Horde had destroyed much of the forest in the surrounding area they couldn't destroy it all. Beneath the great Oaks and younger Birch trees which were common in the new world, crawled two men. They were well camouflaged in pre-collapse military garb and some newer furs. Their skin was covered to stop it being seen by the guards at the edge of the camp which they so expertly moved towards like a pair of shadows in the undergrowth.

Their target had already been chosen. A lone guard who stood leaning on a tree, bored out of his mind and not paying attention to what was making his way towards him. He was only doing guard duty for the extra rations he got, a small amount of meat and bread which was a lot when you didn't get to eat much.

He also wanted to get away from the more extreme guards in the centre of the camp, who beat and killed each other indiscriminately to please their leader. He wore dirty clothes which hadn't been washed in years and were of the pre-collapse kind, brown jeans which were formerly blue and a thick jacket for the cold. He missed the former comfort of the city, his small flat that although was in a bad condition and full of mould was better than the tent he had now. The days watching boring television before work, drinking himself into a stupor and eating cheap but filling fast food seemed like a lifetime away. It was his first time in the countryside and he wished it wasn't.

The two phantoms in the foliage got within a few feet of the man and waited for the right time to strike. The smell from the marshland behind them and the sound of the river moving beside them being their only companions in such a dangerous task and helped to conceal them.

The man made a fatal mistake as he turned his back and began to walk further down the perimeter. One of the phantoms crept out of the brush with his knife in hand before grabbing the man around the neck and squeezing. The knife expertly placed next to his jugular vein.

"If you make a noise you will be dead within a second" he whispered in the man's ear.

They walked backwards through the foliage to a more secluded area away from the tent city, out of earshot and eyesight.

The man was terrified, his eyes darting around thinking it was some kind of joke being played by the other guards in the camp.

He was escorted to a small clearing next to a stinking bog, almost mangrove in composition.

"Who are you and who do you serve?" said one of the masked men crouching in front of him, twirling the knife in between his fingers.

The man began to stutter, trying to find words.

"Ahh... Ahhh... I'm John. We serve Vesh" he was fixated on the knife that was being twirled in front of him.

"Who is this Vesh?, how many people are in his group?"

"He is the leader of the Horde, and I don't

know how many people are in it. Maybe a couple thousand. Who are you people?" he thought that if he answered their questions then maybe they would let him go. He hoped.

"Where is your Horde travelling and for what purpose?" the man with the knife had a blank monotone voice which unsettled the captive.

"I have been told that we are going towards some hills in the south to destroy some dangerous tribes there which caused civilization to collapse in the first place and also to get food. We all come from the city originally and the city has no food any more. All the supplies have been used up. We only scavenge food as we travel now."

After this comment the phantom stopped spinning his knife and just looked at the quivering wreck of a man sat in front of him. The other phantom was behind waiting to finish the job. Holding a club in his hand. They couldn't allow the captive to go back to his master and tell him what had occurred so would have to dispatch him quickly.

It only took a small nod and the club swung down on the man's head, ending his life instantly.

They moved his lifeless corpse to the edge of the fetid bog before rolling him into the green, stinking algae water. As he hit the water a more potent stench of sulphur was released causing the two men to cough and quickly leave the area. The man's body bobbled on the surface, face down and silently drifted amongst the murky water before he began to sink into the mud below.

▲ ▲ ▲

Many miles away to the south a large group of people were camped, waiting for the two scouts to make their way back from the dangerous task they had undertaken. They sat around talking and eating. Some practised archery. The tribal head and leader was talking to some of his trusted men about what the next move will be after the scouts arrive with their information. They had been shadowing the Horde for nearly a week now, trying to find information about them. But all of their attempts had come to nothing thus far.

They were used to moving due to following the Hunter-Gatherer lifestyle which hadn't been seen in Britain for many thousands of years, they moved from place to place with the seasons to hunt the vast supply of boar and deer which frequented the woody hills and valleys of Surrey. Always keeping away from the larger urban areas which they knew were barren and dangerous.

Thy kept to themselves for the most part, their tribe numbering over one-hundred although they were scattered into various smaller tribes which came together for special occasions and festivals or in times of need.

Their tribal leader, a man named Harold. He was brown of hair and blue eyed, he sat in his tent thinking and waiting worriedly.

They could only shadow such a large group for so long before being found and most likely destroyed.

It was a shout that awakened him from his quiet thinking. The two scouts had finally arrived back after a day. Reporting straight to Harold's modest tent to give him their findings about the Horde.

He thanked them for their findings and the dangerous task they had completed. He decided he had no other choice but to follow the only plan he had left. He would have to try and ally with the hill tribes of the Downs to fight the common enemy before them. If not than the scourge would burn its way across the land they held so dear to their hearts.

He told his Thegns the desperate plan

and they all agreed that it was the only way.

They quickly and efficiently made a move, packing their small amount of things and moving through the trees. Some scouts including Harold went ahead to check the path, fearful they may bump into outriders of the Horde.

They were also weary of the strange shadows which lurked in the forest, dark entities which would take the life of anyone who strayed from the group or was unlucky enough to be left behind. They didn't know what these beings were but concluded that they must be ghosts or aliens of some sort which had appeared after the collapse, they had no other explanation. Not knowing that the beings were the elusive Archons.

As they continued to walk the snow was coming down lightly, giving the forest a slight aural glow. They arrived at a small country lane which they followed for a few miles. Wandering through deserted and desolate villages, long void of life. Houses stood empty like tombs, their doors wide open from previous looting and the windows smashed into shards. Curtains of various colours flapped in the breeze. Nature in all cases had begun to consume the former dwellings. Gardens once pristine and mown into barrenness were now full of green and brown life, shrubs growing through the frozen ground the beginnings of a vast forest which would dominate the landscape a few years in the future. Roots which had long been kept in check by the dead powers which had tried to control the world now grew, destroying the tarmac in front of them. In only five short years human colonisation of the planet had been reversed.

Harold had always been conscious of the environment due to his upbringing in the rural countryside and it always gave him joy to see what was once so destructive now disappearing under the sea of trees. The saying his grandfather told him reverberated around his head at such a time; "The strongest trees have the deepest roots."

▲ ▲ ▲

It wasn't long before the large group was in sight of the cloud covered Downs and they began snaking their way through the trees, up the chalky banks following narrow, well-worn deer paths and older footpaths until they reached the summit and could look down on the Fortress. They made their camp away from the precipice in order to not be seen by the sentries guarding and patrolling the prickly palisade wall which skirted around the edge of the settlement and the guard towers which could be seen at the main gate. They kept quiet and as night began to fall they could hear singing and other merriment rising from the settlement, as well as a large bonfire which was letting of a large amount of flickering light which illuminated the surrounding countryside.

In Harold's tent they pondered over how to make the first point of contact with the settlement below them.

"Why don't we all just march down there and knock on the gate" said Sigurd, one of Harold's Thegns and also his younger brother.

"Don't be ridiculous, what if they open fire on us thinking we are trying to raid or besiege the village. We know these hill tribes like to keep to themselves and aren't afraid to deal with threats. We need to show them we aren't a threat" said Harold, authoritatively.

It would be a constant debate of ideas flowing from everyone in the tribe, getting heated at points. It was only after the soothing and sweet voice of Harold's wife, Alice, was heard when they came to a decision.

"Why doesn't Harold write a letter directed to the leader of the village, telling them that we are no threat and only want to speak to them about grave matters concerning both of our people and their ultimate survival. You could wrap the letter around a rock or stone and throw it over the wall. I'm sure that someone would find it the next day if it landed in the right spot. And if they don't find it then we can always send a messenger, although that would be more dangerous."

They all nodded and agreed with her. A volunteer was asked to do the perilous job of making his way to the palisade and throwing the important letter over it, and their was no shortage of those raising their hand to do the job. The volunteer being chosen was Sigurd who was only happy at doing such a dangerous task for his tribe and people.

The letter was written, paper and pen

was not in short supply as it was used to homeschool the many children in the group before it was wrapped around a large piece of common flint which was abundant on the Downs and tied on with nettle cordage which had been saved since the late days of summer.

The letter was written in good handwriting and said;

"To the leader and/or leaders of this village.

I write this letter to you in great haste, we are Nomadic folk who wish to speak about grave tidings which face both of our people and their ultimate survival. Please give us a sign or make contact with us as quickly as possible. We are situated on the hill above your settlement and number some one-hundred twenty people.

Signed Harold, of Harold's Folk"

He then made a small cut in his thumb and allowed the blood to settle on the paper.

It was only mere minutes before Sigurd was creeping down the hillside towards the settlement. The soil and chalk crumbled under his feet as he tried to walk but ended up sliding down a lot of the embankment before getting to the wooded base of the hills and gained better footing. The darkness was terrifying and he worried about the dark entities which were known to hide amongst the shadows in glades. He fumbled through the trees before falling a short distance into what once would have been a field of some size which had now gone fallow and was covered in a thick layer of cropped grass. He could hear the inhabitants singing and being merry from within the settlement, folk songs being sung and the shouts of children playing and having fun.

As he walked along the edge of the field he was taken by surprise when he could see a large tower In the a few hundred metres in front of him. He dived onto the cold, frozen ground, scuffing his elbows and knees in the process which made him wince at the pain.

He scanned the tower to the best of his abilities to see if it was being occupied by a sentry but in the darkness it was nearly impossible, only the warm glow of a candle which radiated out from the window told him it might be occupied. He waited still and silently for a few minutes but saw no movement so began crawling like a lizard towards the tower and what he hoped was the main gate. Once he was within a few dozen metres he could see that it was in ruins, with crumbling rocks and other natural debris surrounding it, but it was occupied with shrubs and vines all around which helped camouflage and keep it company. He looked at it with wonder before continuing on his mission towards the settlement.

The nervousness he had as we went past it slowly, crawling on the cold ground made him sweat slightly. At any moment he thought that he would be caught, that a light would appear in front of him and a hand would grab his neck and drag him away. But all went to plan as he continued moving.

He got within distance of the wall and could see the huge, cut logs of the palisade which looked like spiked stakes jutting up into the heavens.
"Am I in the Iron Age?" he thought to himself, remembering what he was taught many years before about the subject and the pictures of hill forts he would see in his school textbooks.
Along the wall he could see the silhouettes of a few guardsmen moving along it in the small amount of moonlight and could hear them chattering amongst themselves in hushed tones. He only moved when they moved to make himself more hidden and it worked as they went about their patrol without any

fuss. One of the sentries stood for a moment, looking out over the empty space in front of him and made Sigurd, who was halfway between crawling and stopping, hold his breath in panic induced anxiety thinking that he had been spotted. But a few seconds past and the sentry continued walking on to the next part of the wall.

Sigurd let out a sigh of relief before snaking further onwards.

After what seemed like hours he reached the bottom of the wall and knelt before taking the medium sized piece of flint out of his pocket. Feeling the wall it was sticky with some kind of tar-like substance which he guessed was to stop the wood from rotting away quickly in the humid climate. He waited patiently until the sentry was far enough away before making his way down the wall towards the gate which was noticeably further out than the rest of the wall. Once he got to the main tower he took a few steps away from the wall and as silently as he could he launched the rock over the wall. It made a slight whistle as it flew over and only just missed clipping the top of the palisade which would have been disastrous he thought. His heart was in his mouth until he heard it hit the ground on the other side with a slight bump before he felt relieved. The easy part was now done, the hard part was about to begin. As soon as it hit the ground he was back onto the cold earth and beginning to crawl back to the wooded slopes and his tribe.

▲ ▲ ▲

Within the walls of the Fortress things were beginning to wind down as the night turned into the early hours of the morning. The people began making there way back to there dwellings for a rest before the next day of work and toil.

Cyril took a walk with some jugs of ale in each hand for the sentry's who couldn't come to the festivities and were instead stuck on the cold, wind chilled walls with the job of protecting the settlement from any and all threats. Each of the dozen or so of them were happy at the sight of a tankard of ale which Cyril handed out to to them, even going back to collect more as his two hands couldn't carry all of them in one go, their gratefulness was plain to see at such a gesture as it helped make the boring job more pleasant and warmed them up.

Once he finished doing his rounds he began to walk back to his house which was nestled in the centre of the settlement, looking forward to his bed and the warmth it would bring.

He walked with a content feeling that the world was finally getting better, the people were happy and the future was prosperous before his daze was cut short as he tripped. Looking down he realised it was a large rock of some kind. He looked at it puzzled for a moment, the streets were always cleared of debris and other matter so their would never be a rock lying there. Picking it up he noticed the paper and cordage and began to untie it as he walked, intrigued. It was a letter but he couldn't read it in the low light.

He could see his house was glowing from the candles and fireplace which shined through the windows as he walked up the main path and closed the wrought iron gate behind him. He entered through the patio doors and into the main room which was occupied by Anderson and his wife at that time.

As he entered he went straight towards the fire to read the note without a word to Anderson who sat next to the fire. "Have you just collected some post? I thought they stopped sending mail five years ago" said Anderson.

Cyril began reading and his face began to drop.

"Go and wake up Earl now and get some men together to go to the walls immediately" Cyril shouted.

Anderson was like a statue before his military head came to the surface and he rushed off towards the main door grabbing his shield and spear on the way.

Chapter III

A night of anxiety led to the beginning of a bright but freezing cold morning which was exacerbated by a painful wind chill which blew in from the southern coast. The Fortress was in a state of frenzy with people going here, there and everywhere. Women and children making their way towards the centre of the village and most of the able-bodied men armed and armoured on the walls and other important features.

Cyril was dressed in his mail with his Seax at his side and beside him stood one of his trusted Thegns called Henrik, who carried his standard which fluttered nicely in the frigid breeze. On the black banner sat a bright white Ingwaz rune at the centre. It was an ancient symbol which Cyril felt an affinity to after first seeing it.

Earl and Anderson were also dressed in their armour and carried their standards with them. A total of thirty-five men and also Rebecca walked through the main gate and began walking up towards the mysterious host who were camped at the summit of one of the many hills which made the Downs, and who wanted to meet them. In the heavy armour they wore it was a hard trek, all up hill, hemmed in from all sides by the hibernating trees who were bare of leaf and who's branches reached over and met in the centre of what once was the main road through the ancient village.

The road itself was icy and covered In the autumns leaf litter which was covered in a thick frost and added an extra slippery layer on top of the ice below. It wasn't long before they got a small plateau in the road on which they stopped and waited. Hands on Seax handles in fear that it was a trap from those who wanted to meet them.

▲ ▲ ▲

Amongst the trees a spotter was watching the entourage and their every move. He chirped like a bird to alert a man who was waiting further down the tree line. The bird sounds made its way half way up the hill before a runner made his way to Harold's tent.

He was sat in his pristine armour and furs awaiting the call.

"Good, Good" he said as he jumped out of his seat and made his way out of the tent. The runner, a young man named Osmond who before the collapse ran professionally in marathons, was told to go and meet Cyril's entourage and ask them if they are peaceful and wished to speak to Harold.

A nervousness began to spread around the camp although they believed the Hill Tribes to be honourable they still didn't trust anyone as it was easy to deceive people in the New World they called home.

Osmond made his way down the hill quickly but watching his step on the slippery ground, he was a tall man of fair complexion. His hair almost white it was so blonde. He walked as he got closer to the group of individuals waiting with their flags fluttering in the wind. He didn't want to take Cyril and his people by surprise by running.

"Greetings, I am a messenger from Harold. He asks if you are peaceful and willing to speak to him about the matters which are of grave importance, if not we are willing to leave your land without any trouble"
The messenger was standing a few metres away and was very clear In his way of speaking. Having a certain eloquence with his accent.

"We are peaceful and want to speak to him" said Cyril bluntly, still keeping an eye on the treeline for any signs of an ambush.

"Certainly, please wait a few moments" said Osmond before smiling, bowing and turning around and jogging precariously back towards where he had come from. His feet slipping more than a few times as he climbed back up the incline of the hill. Cyril and the others waited with hands on sword handles. All seemed quiet around them and if an ambush was going to occur it would be now they thought.

Harold along with his Thegns were ready to march down the hill. His most trusted Thegns, Wulf, Sigurd and Vendel carried some gifts in their arms including furs and venison. Items of extreme value in the eyes of the Nomadic people.

Ten men from Harold's tribe began walking down the slippery slope. With

Harold at the front followed by his Thegns, behind them was the messenger and the tribal Druid who had a group of his own Thegns with him. They all dressed in their best armour and furs. Like a spectacle that could have been taken from a history book on the Bronze or Iron Age. Their weapons were not exquisite but practical, Axes and bows being the most common but others had knives and antique swords which were at their sides.

The two groups faced each other on the plateau of the road and a silence fell between them. It was Harold who broke the almost deafly silence;
"Greetings, I am Harold, my tribe sits on the hill above your settlement. We have bought you some gifts which we hope will be to your liking. Furs to keep you warm during the cold winter and some meat to keep you from going hungry" he had a warm, friendly smile as he pointed at the items which Sigurd and Vendel

held higher so that Cyril and his people could get a better look.

"The reason why me and my people wish to speak to you is due to a substantial threat which we have uncovered and which is making its way towards you and your settlement. It is getting closer every day. A huge group of people are pillaging from the cities north of here, we have already seen them enslave many smaller tribes and people who were living in peace much like yourselves. They call themselves the Horde and from what my scouts have told me they number in the thousands. They grow their numbers by using terrible slavery and exploitation of the people they conquer but many others have joined them of their own free will it seems. People of unhonourable, psychotic backgrounds. Me and my people are Nomadic, we do not want to be tied to the land but want to live upon it in peace and keep to ourselves, although our peoples do know of each other from sightings in this area over the last few years we have never had any trouble and we believe you are people of honourable character."

Cyril kept silent as Harold spoke, listening closely to what he said, in front of him he saw a man very much like himself. A man carrying the burden of his people in his mind and soul.
"I am Cyril and these are my Thegns, Earl of the Trundle standing to my left and Anderson of Blackdown standing to my right." They both nodded at Harold, "This is my wife Rebecca" she smiled pleasantly, "I thank you graciously for the gifts. The news you bring us is extremely concerning although we thank you for alerting us, we respect people of good character such as yourself and find your way of life noble. I think it would be better if we spoke in a more secure area. Would you follow us down to the settlement?"

Harold waited for a second, glancing at his Thegns who didn't complain before making his decision.

"Of course, as long as my people can also make their way down into your settlement as well" he said.

"Your people are very welcome, they can set their tents on the village green. We will get the fires going and have a feast tonight for both of our people" replied Cyril in a friendly manner.

He took a step forward, arm outstretched and shook Harold's hand in a symbolic gesture before they began walking towards the wooden gate of the Fortress. Osmond began making the trek back up the hill to give the humble people of Harold's tribe the good news to collect their things and meet down in the village.

They entered through the commanding gate which opened slowly with its hinges creaking painfully. Cyril and his people walked in front with Harold and his small group following them behind. Harold was physically impressed by the size of the wall and gate which loomed over the group as they walked through it. He hadn't seen anything like it.

The village was busier than usual with the sound of the blacksmith hammering out new swords, arrowheads, axeheads, spearheads and other more mundane but important items closer to the centre of the village. Each hit on the anvil creating the distinctive ring of metal upon metal. The carpenters were also plying their trade, making shields and handles for spears and axes at an astounding rate. Bowyers and fletchers nearby making Bows and arrows. The amount of industry surprised Harold and his men. They were used to creating their own tools and weapons from scratch or scavenging them on their many and frequent hunts and movements across the countryside. "Where do you get all the materials to create so many tools?" he said surprised, and directing the question at Cyril. "We scavenge most of the materials we need. We recycle them into things into workable sizes and then reuse them for tools. If we find anything worth smelting then the scavengers bring it back and we turn into a variety of things. We don't mind using old world tools but we found a lot of them broke soon after we began building the Fortress so we decided that we could make better tools ourselves. Same with our clothes, and wood is easy to come by. Most of the cars and other vehicles in the village were used to repair buildings by using the sheet metal or to create stronger parts to the fortifications" replied Cyril, proud of what his people had created in such a small amount of time.

"We are Hunter-gatherers and also scavenge but only if we can't make the items ourselves. Stone and wood are the most important but steel is nice to have if you can get it" said Harold.

Harold also noticed how clean the streets and buildings were, and the people who looked very much like his own and to his surprise looked happy and thriving in such difficult conditions which followed the great collapse.

Walking past the village hall was the remnants of the nights revelry which was being cleaned away quite quickly. Cyril stopped them and introduced Harold and told them about the feast which would take place later that evening for their guests. The tables and chairs which would have been cleared away were left and the braziers were relit for later on in the day.

The news spread fast about the new visitors and most of the village turned out to greet them in a friendly way, from their doorsteps, windows or in the street as they walked past.

Carrying on past the bustling crafts people they quickly made it to Cyril and Rebecca's house and into the small, warm study.

Harold sat down on the large curved backed seat before taking his helmet off and placing it alongside him. His Thegns doing the same but instead they held theirs.

"Would you like some food and drink Harold?" offered Cyril, the sound of the kettle boiling in the kitchen.

"I thank you for the offer but no thank you" he replied courteously.

Cyril sat down, facing Harold across the desk and made himself comfortable.

"This horde you speak about, where is it located exactly?, we occasionally have groups of raiders who come into our territory but it is never anything serious and we chase them off before they can take anything in most cases" Cyril began scribbling notes on a piece of paper he had resting on his desk.

"We first spotted them In the North Downs and the hills of Surrey but when we got closer to them they became hostile, so we kept our distance and shadowed them for a while before moving further south into your territory. They are certainly moving in this direction and from my scouts reports they have a hatred of country folk such as ourselves." Harold could tell Cyril was a man of the country from his accent, and also from his manners, which lacked in most former urbanites.

"We have time to prepare then?"

"Yes, they are at least a few days from here in distance. Due to the size of the Horde it could be more than a few days before they get here but it is certain they move in this direction."

"Good. I will put my men to work building extra fortifications and other defences. I suggest we make an alliance of sorts. With our numbers put together we won't have enough men to be equal with how many they have but I imagine we are better trained than the rabble they are made of."

"Very much so" Harold replied, "from my reports the Horde has no trained force. Just an armed rabble who use their numbers to overwhelm their opponents, then subjugating them or executing them. We could tell from the start that they were not from this area. Their manners and ways aren't of the country. They destroy and pillage anything that gets in there way and have no respect for the beautiful land and nature we dwell alongside."

Out of the window the people of Harold's tribe could be seen moving through the village and towards the green. They carried all of their worldly possessions with them. Bags filled to the brim on backs, pots and pans clanging together while others had the duty of carrying large tents made from old world materials and also animal hides which had been stitched together. Rebecca could be seen standing at the front with Elfin in her arms directing the movements of the newcomers all the while speaking to Harold's wife.

They continued their debate, getting to know each other. No quarrels being made on either side and many similarities were found between them, from world-view and religious beliefs to the daily musings of family men. Their Thegns also talked amongst themselves about tactics and other interesting topics. About their families and what life was like for them.

Cyril stood, still talking to Harold and walked to an oak desk which was perched under one of the old square windows in the study. He opened the dusty drawer in which contained an elegantly designed short Seax, created only shortly after the collapse happened. It was ornate, with beautiful designs reminiscent of brambles and other plants inlayed in steel and copper twisting over the scabbard and handle, the blade was still sharp, practical and well oiled. He collected it, holding it by the scabbard before closing the drawer and walked back to his main desk at the centre of the room. He placed it delicately in front of Harold before sitting back down and sipping the mug of hot pine needle tea.

"A gift for you Harold, I hope a long and prosperous peace between our people" Harold looked at the Seax with slight amazement at the craftsmanship, before picking it up and feeling its weight in his hand before unsheathing it and checking the blade and its razor sharpness.

"A fine blade indeed. I thank you and wish the same for our peoples."

Chapter IV

"What do you mean you found him floating in the bog? Who killed him and for what purpose? I want answers." Vesh shouted at the blubbering mess of a man stood below his makeshift throne which was made from wood and scrap metal bolted together. The man was one of his many lieutenants and the leader of the Hordes makeshift camp sentry unit. He was kneeling in the mud not daring to look at his leader out of timidity at such an embarrassing occasion.

"My lord, we don't know who killed him but he does have a wound to his head which leads us to believe that he was hit in some way" he stuttered which elicited a small laugh from Vesh.

"I put my trust in you and you failed me, so now I shall fail you." Vesh clicked his fingers and two masked men, stepped out from behind his throne grabbed the lieutenant from behind, grabbing the cuff of his unclean shirt and began dragging him away towards the gallows which had been created from one of the trees which had yet to be cut down or burnt.

"Please! Please! NO!" he screamed in protest, which got no answer and proved to be to no avail. All it got him was a punch in the mouth for his trouble which shattered his teeth and filled his mouth with blood. His screams became muffled as he struggled to spit out the broken fragments of teeth mixed with warm, metallic tasting blood. He fidgeted weakly in the vice grip of the two towering guards, trying to escape their clutches but was to weak and they smirked at his futile attempt with psychotic glee. In the struggle his shoulder dislocated with a disgusting popping sound. The agony it caused became almost unbearable and was exacerbated by the effect of him being dragged through the stodgy, clinging mud.

The large oak came into view, hack marks and black smoke stains in its furrowed trunk from attempts to chop and burn it down. On one of the lower branches hung a rope with a noose on the end. It swung slightly in the breeze, almost like it was waiting and ready for the job in hand.

At this sight the man passed out from shock and fell face down, the guards were caught by surprise at the weight of his unconscious body and he slipped from their grip. He dropped into the mud like an anchor, causing a splash of stagnant mud to spray in every direction. They lifted him back up and slapped him across the face a dozen times. He didn't awake. A few shouts and another guard jogged to the area with a bucket of stinking bog water which he doused over the man's face.

He awoke with a startle and began immediately trying to escape with laughs and jeers from the crowd over hundreds which had formed to see the grim spectacle.

Underneath the branch was a rusted oil barrel with a set of steps next to it. Another masked guard stood waiting as the executioner to put the strong rope around the man's fragile neck.

He still struggled and more henchmen had to be found to lift him up the steps and onto the barrel to face his fate. All the while his leader, Vesh, who had exited his throne made his way towards the gallows to watch proceedings. Smiling all the while.

The rope went over his head and was pulled tight to fit snugly around his neck by the grinning executioner.

His breathing became stressed and heavy at the tightness as the rope was yanked closed and his chest was raising and lowering, faster and faster. His arm flapped trying to claw at the rope but it was too tight and he couldn't get his fingers underneath the rough twine.

"Any last words?" Vesh said, sarcastically.

"No" the man replied with a cry, looking to the ground. His brain trying and failing to try and comprehend what was happening.

"Good" Vesh nodded and the nearest masked guard kicked the barrel underneath the man's feet and sent it into the mud with a crash. The man fell as gravity took hold and his body went limp before he began to struggle, his body thrashed around as his life began to leave it. The branch moved up and down like a macabre see-saw. It didn't take long before the thrashing became a small twitch as his muscles used up the energy left in them and the nerves still fired for a few minutes after death. His eyes rolled into the back of his head and his tongue fell limply from his mouth.

Vesh was ecstatic like a child getting a new toy, enjoying every second of the grim exercise in front of him.

He left the man's lifeless body swinging from the branch, dozens of flies already began landing on the fresh corpse to lay their eggs. The corpse would be a warning to the others in his Horde who dared defy or not follow what he believed was his divine command.

His happiness was short lived before he went back into the usual anger. He decided to implement his next plan of attack against his enemies and assembled a large group of his followers at the base of the ancient oak. Some of those gathered looked pale and nauseous as their eyes peered at the corpse hanging in front of them. Swaying in front of them like a pendulum. Others weren't bothered at the sight, seeing death many times before. Especially after the great collapse.

His voice squeaked as he spoke; "I have assembled you all because we are going to do a scouting trip to find out who killed the sentry. I also know we are close to the Yokel settlements now. It is about time we wiped the savages of the face of the earth once and for all."

Shouts of agreement came from the group, many barely understood what he was saying and just agreed out of fear, some of them being former criminals and others who were released from a prison just before the final collapse. Seeing Vesh as their ultimate saviour from the barren walls and cells.

"Some of the Yokels may change their minds and join us, after realising their backwards and disgusting ways are no match to us. They can help us lay concrete over this vast, muddy mess they call home... Follow me!" he shouted before being handed his thin armour vest of mail, which was rusted and in need of repairs, by one of the many bodyguards always around him, and a small claw hammer which he kept on his belt. His main weapon of choice being a large, two handed sledgehammer.

They left the tent city before heading out into the forested hills and heathlands of the Surrey countryside with vigour and hatred.

▲ ▲ ▲

The land was empty as they moved slowly through it. Trees and shrubs had begun colonising every patch of soil for as far as the eye could see. The roads were crumbling into dust from the roots which grew beneath them. Abandoned vehicles littered the road, most had their doors open and were looted years beforehand. Rust had set in on the bodywork and some were burnt out. The large group cursed each step they took in the difficult, hilly terrain. Every house they passed was thoroughly searched in hopes of finding gold or any other precious but useless items, while other valuable tools for survival were left by the ignorant raiders. Some of the houses were set on fire for fun, especially those that looked more rural-like. Vesh exacted a tithe of everything found and added to his vast collection of gems and other useless commodities which he stored in his tent and used to award loyal followers. Every house they came to was long abandoned and showed no sign of life for many years. The occasional skeleton gave an idea of what had happened to the inhabitants. Most of the buildings had already been ransacked and had foliage and other plants growing out of them. Branches reached out of broken windows while holes in the collapsing roofs gave way to tree trunks and other limbs.

A young red Fox sleeping snugly, taking advantage of the derelict building for shelter out of the cold and wet was startled as the door came crashing in next to it. With a yelp it took off at speed and through the empty smashed window chased by the two, almost as surprised men who wanted to kill and skin it as a trophy and to its meat for food. The wily young fox got the better of them and disappeared into the brush like a shot, escaping from their clutches and knives.

They gave chase and struggled through the thick natural foliage and burst through to a small clearing in which were many shelters made from branches and other tree litter. Dispersed in between being the burnt out remains of firepits. The ash from them long since burnt out.
"HEY!… We found something!" shouted one of the men back to the group which was loitering in the road.

Vesh wandered amongst the ruins of Harold's camp, looking into the shelters for clues to where they could be but their was no trace of living and hadn't been for a few weeks at least. He began to feel his rage bubbling to the surface and tried to destroy the nearest wooden teepee to him but failed. The wood held strong and he kicked it in protest.

"Look at how they live, vile, they actually take enjoyment in living like this. Without glass, or concrete. Such awful savages, sleeping on the bare ground like animals" he complained, spitting as he walked.
"Burn it all. This is my land now and I won't have mess like this plaguing valuable building space." he screamed and his henchmen jumped at the opportunity for more destruction.

At his command the shelters began to be set alight with flint or lighters which were still common to find in the desolate world. The dry nature of the inside of the shelters allowed them to go up like sparklers and it was very soon before the whole area was a bright, burning mass. Dark smoke billowed up towards the white clouds above and the heat became near unbearable for the group who began moving from whence they came. The fire spread over the ground and many trees which were rich with sap after the autumn joined the deathly crescendo of flames. As the wind blew it spread further and further, the houses were next to go up in an orange glow and then the bone dry heather on the heath further down the trail. The scale of the fire left an orange glow on the horizon as the group of raiders made their way back to the tent city with their loot.

"Tomorrow at dawn we will begin to move south and take what is rightfully ours from the Yokels who occupy it". His manic laugh gave them all shivers.

Chapter V

A group of volunteers stood in the cold morning air which blanketed the land of Sussex, they had been assembled by Cyril and Harold and came from both of the two tribes who currently occupied the Fortress. Five of them being Cyril's men and the other five being from Harold's tribe.

"We need four volunteers" explained Cyril, "For an important reconnaissance mission to the south coast. We've decided that three from our tribe and one from Harold's will go. You will have to test the coastal area and sea at Selsey, checking for radiation or any other pollutants and to see if the area is vacant. Any questions?", nobody spoke

"Okay, choose amongst yourself to who is going"

The group began talking and chose the four men fairly quickly.

The first man who was chosen was Wulf,

he was an expert tracker was the volunteer from Harold's tribe. More men from the Nomads volunteered but weren't needed for the small but dangerous expedition. From Cyril's side the three volunteers stepped forward. Claude, who knew the area they were travelling to very well due to his upbringing by the coast. Otto, the youngest of the group who begged and insisted to his older comrades that he be allowed to go on the expedition, his wish being granted on the account that he didn't do anything stupid which put himself or the others at danger. The last volunteer being a man named Arthur, a quiet and humble individual who, before the great collapse, was a scientist working in the field of chemistry. He was selected due to his small but important knowledge on radiation.

They all packed a few essentials for the journey. Food to last a day or two and each had their Seax and shields with them, apart from Wulf who carried an axe and a bow and refused to bring a shield, claiming it was to cumbersome. Arthur also carried a large Geiger counter in a box which hung from his neck. It was a valuable and found in a huge house which was raided many years before.

They set off early in the morning after saying farewell to their families and friends, many of them coming out to see them off on their dangerous journey. Their shields slung over their backs jingled against the mail they wore.

Cyril stood watching from the gate, waving as they wandered underneath and appeared out the other side. They all thought to themselves in worry, not knowing what could happen on the expedition and wondering if they would ever see their families again but as soon as these thoughts began they ended as they started their journey into the hinterland.

Like most days during that time of the year the ground was frozen solid and the trees lay bare of leaf apart from the conifers which were dotted around in large numbers. The countryside seemed barren and empty as they headed south, through the great chalk escarpment and onto the plain below it. The ground became more flat and the remains of fields surrounded them, formerly ploughed but now covered with a sea of bare saplings and shrubs. Gorse and Broom had colonised vast tracts of what was now urban wasteland amongst the ruins of villages and which with each passing year grew a little larger and became a step closer to rewilding the land back to how it was all those thousands of years before.

They were weary on the road for other humans more than anything else. They knew falling into the wrong hands could mean serious injury or death. They kept to the side of the road and gave areas of forest and deep woodland a wide berth. The talk of Thorburn and the tiger put them on edge and their eyes darted at any moving shadows in the brush. Local Wolves who prowled through the hills and valleys of the Downs were less of a threat to them as they moved in a group.

"What did you all do before the collapse?" said Wulf to nobody In particular, trying to spark up conversation with the others in the group. A small silence ensued as they all waited for someone else to answer the question.

"I was a builder down Chichester way and Selsey. It was hard work and I miss it sometimes but life is better now. We are more free and don't have to worry about mundane things like money" said Claude, reminiscing slightly as he spoke. Remembering all of those back breaking days pouring cement for some new, ugly building which blotted the landscape. He spoke of his colleagues and life before and they all remembered their own lives which had changed so much, for the better.

"I worked as a lab assistant for a company which created chemicals which were then sent to the military for whatever means they used them for. It was all top secret work but being a lowly ranked assistant I never knew what they used it for. Some guys from a small detachment of the Army would come and collect what they needed every few weeks without speaking to anyone and we weren't allowed to speak to them either. I think they were using it for some kind of military black project, we will never know now." Arthur spoke softly and everyone listened intently.

"What about you young one?" said Wulf to Otto.

"I was still in school when all this happened. I guess I was one of the lucky ones. My parents and siblings all died early on in the collapse from the illness, I was the only one left from my class at school. The funny aspect of it all was I knew that this would all happen one day, the collapse I mean, but everyone else thought I was mad for saying it. I prepared for it and was mocked, even my own family mocked me for it but I was the only one to survive in the end. After a few months of wandering the empty countryside with a group of raiders trying to survive I ran away and found Cyril and Rebecca at The Trundle and they allowed me to live there with them and the few others at that time. When I met them their were only fifteen people in our tribe."

It went silent for a while and all that could be heard was the soft thud of their boots walking along the cracking asphalt. "What about you Wulf, what did you do before the collapse?" said Claude.

He was silent for a few moments, moving the question around in his head before answering.

"I did many things. I moved from place to place with my wife and daughter, doing odd jobs for people for money before we settled down in Guildford, I never liked it there though. It was far to Urban for me. Once the collapse came I got out of their as quick as I could but my wife and daughter didn't make it." He stopped, the sadness was plain to see as he looked down to his feet as he walked before he brought himself back. "My sister was married to Harold so I joined them as I had no one else to stay with. We started hunting and gathering just after that, the more simple way of living is much better, we are free now."

They all agreed with him.

They walked for a few hours in the cold, desolate but natural landscape. Not seeing a single soul as they made good progress through the hills and into the flat plateau that rested beneath them. The hills began to disappear in the distance as they walked through village and field. Subtle aspects of urbanism could be seen poking through the foliage as they got closer to the ruins of Chichester. They had travelled for a few hours and were looking for a well deserved break at the Trundle which could be seen looming in the distance, before they carried on their journey towards the coast.

The outskirts of Chichester were deserted with the rusted remains of vehicles littering the road. Trees which were planted as ornamentation between street lights and still stood firm while the buildings all around them began to crumble.

An ambulance stood in the middle of the main road at an angle suggesting it must have stopped in a rush and stood with its doors hanging open and its contents long pillaged of its rare and sought after medical supplies.

They were taking a risk travelling through urban areas due to the threat of raiders but their time was limited and nobody had decided to live in the ruins of the small city for years.

Here and there a skeleton lay on the cold pavement, the remnants of one of those many who didn't make it once civilisation fell.

Long since picked clean of valuables and flesh and their bones bleached by the hot summer sun.

They moved through Summersdale on the outskirts of Chichester, with its large suburban housing and towards the centre of that ancient city which was growing smaller every passing year.

Everywhere looked the same with plants taking back the land and growing from every fleck of dirt that could be found.

Fences were mostly lying face down on the concrete with the plants in former gardens clawing their way into the outside world.

Claude led them, knowing the city like the back of his hand. Taking them down the many shortcuts and twittens which were dotted all around. The centre of the city was desolate and deserted. Reminiscent of Stalingrad during the height of the Second World War. Buildings collapsing, burnt out and empty. Shops which were filled with people ransacked and like skeletons. The cathedral a ruins. It's gothic architecture still standing in places but most being piled up in the centre of the nave due to the collapse of the spire five years before. The Yew tree which sat in the churchyard had grown substantially in contrast to its stone neighbour which once shadowed it, and now towered above the arch it lived beside. Covering most of the sparse gravestones in darkness as its poisonous sap dripped onto the frozen dirt.

An eerie silence filled the void of the

streets which would have once been bustling, noises of diesel spewing buses and other vehicles gone. The constant buzz of planes flying above gone. It gave them a certain relaxed feeling as the only noise that could be heard was their feet and the gentle sound of the wind blowing through the empty streets.

Breaking the normal protocols they decided to inspect the inside of the ruined cathedral out of a feeling of curiosity. It was very much as they expected. Anything deemed of value was long pillaged. A huge chasm which would have once been covered by stone thousands of tonnes in weight was open to the elements above them.
The stone itself had begun to turn a bright green as moss and lichen grew in the moist and humid conditions. They looked up at the sky and it made them feel dizzy with a feeling that the walls were going to fall in.

In the centre was the immense pile of rubble which had been left when the spire fell in on itself. They didn't bother to climb it. Many old memorials to rich patrons and the deceased still covered the walls which hadn't been blasted into oblivion by the spire, and most were unreadable from the layer of lichen and ivy that covered them after five years in the elements. All of those people long forgotten to the dust of time. It was nature which had moved in to the ruins and in the cracks grass and herbs had colonised and grew in the small ecosystem which existed in the enclosed space.

They were quiet as they moved amongst the ruins, almost waiting for someone or something to jump out and scare them but the silence was all around. Some glints of coloured light filtered through the smashed stained glass windows, many of which were smeared with a thick layer of soot which had been deposited from the great fire.

The stone effigy's of former bishops and other church officials were not damaged but had their sarcophagus lids removed, which they surmised was caused by pillagers hoping to find old treasure or other objects they deemed valuable in the caskets. Only skulls peered out, and some were no longer in humanoid shape but instead a layer of dust rested at the bottom of the sarcophagi they inhabited. After a few minutes they left the ruins behind as they continued their journey towards the coast with added haste.

Otto was becoming more and more twitchy as he looked around and kept seeing shadows out of his peripheral vision in windows and doorways which would quickly disappear when he glanced at them. His eyes darted around like two laser's. He wondered if he was going insane or just seeing things.

"Otto, can you see the shadows?" whispered Claude as they continued walking.

"Yes, they are in all of the windows and doorways"

"Just keep walking and calm down, they won't do anything if we are in a group"

"Okay, Okay" he looked down, watching Claude's feet to see where they were going as they walked out of the city.

The entities were numerous as always in the ruins of cities like they were in the darkness of the forest, always waiting for someone to stumble upon them so they could feed on their valuable energy and life essence. Hiding in the portals of doorways or windows, the corners of abandoned buildings and other dark spaces before they could ambush those who were least expecting it. They were beings of extreme patience while looking for lonely stranglers before causing them extreme anxiety and fear and then dispatching them swiftly and efficiently.

The others walked quickly, keeping their eyes adjusted on the distant countryside which they could see peeking through the buildings on either side of the blocked road. There was a change of feeling in the air as they exited the urban area and were quickly surrounded by the trees and fields but they still refused to look back out of fear of the shadows following them and it was many minutes and half a mile before they stopped walking and had a rest.

The road behind them was empty and they hadn't been stalked by the shadows to their great relief.
"I thought those shadows were an Urban legend mothers told their children if they misbehaved" Otto said, wiping his brow free of nervous sweat.
"Most legends come from truth. Why do you think we always walk around in

groups when we are away from the Fortress" said Claude, giggling slightly at Otto's fear.

"They won't ever attack you if you travel in a group, they hunt people who are travelling alone. If you hadn't been with us your drained corpse would be lying in the dust by now. Your fear is what they feed on."

Wulf and Arthur smirked as Otto looked around still slightly anxious at what he had just saw.

"Come on let's keep going, we aren't to far from the Trundle. We can have a rest and lunch there" said Claude before starting off on the empty road again.

They continued their journey, Northwards now towards the Trundle which was stooped above the surrounding land. It was only a short journey but took a while as they travelled through the countryside to reach its steep sides. Lucky that the ground was hard and frozen, any rain and the sides of the hill made climbing up the narrow track nearly impossible. The track they took was well worn from foot traffic and they unfurled the flag of the Fortress and held it up as they walked forward towards the wooden gate to show the sentry's that they were friendly. The rule was shoot first and ask questions later when it came to defence. They didn't want to be accidentally felled by an arrow.

The gate opened slowly and they passed through the portal it created passing into the open space behind and were warmly welcomed and greeted by some of the inhabitants, many of whom they hadn't seen for what seemed like an age.

"We have some bad news" said Claude to the group who had come out of the many huts and other structures which were located across the large hilltop.

"You are all going to have to pack up your things and head to the Fortress because trouble is brewing and we need all the hands we can get to help fight it off."

"When will we have to leave?" said an elderly gentlemen, with nods of agreement from some of the others assembled.

"Tomorrow. We are heading to the coast to check the water for radiation and then we will be heading back so we can all travel back to the Fortress together, I will tell you more once we have had a bite to eat."

The group sat on down and began eating some food, stew and dumplings, which was brought to them by the inhabitants. They chatted about how life was at the Fortress. Wulf was introduced to and thanked them for the food which he quickly gulped and washed down with some weak home-brewed ale.

Claude told them what he knew about

Vesh and the horde, Wulf adding to his report. The news spread quickly amongst the people of the Trundle, many of whom were only happy and willing to fight for their survival and freedom or die in the process.

The group of men noticed that they could see people collecting their things already, putting them together on carts. Most of the people had a sad look on their faces after being told the alarming news. Some retired to their houses after being told and didn't come back out.

They finished their meal and drank up the rest of the beer before thanking the people again for their hospitality. They walked slowly to the gate before leaving the large settlement. The weather was still cold as noon arrived and the wind chill on top of the hill was biting to any exposed skin.

They Walked down the side of the muddy hill and through the woodland which surrounded it they came across the fabled house where their tribe began those few years before. The cottage was all but a burnt husk of its former self, the only difference being the large stone cairn, layered in moss, which stood in a clearing next to the building. It was built very soon after the collapse, a memorial to Robert. A man who they were all told sacrificed himself in battle for the tribe and if he hadn't then they all would have perished.

Once again they were back on the road heading south towards the coast with full bellies and making the decision to give the skeleton-like city a wide berth. They knew it wasn't far but still walked hastily, fearful of the setting sun which would cloak the land in darkness in only a few short hours.

▲ ▲ ▲

As they got closer and closer to the coast they could feel the change in temperature and the smell of salt in the air became apparent.

The small coastal town itself was abandoned, as all urban areas were in the New World, but it had begun to decay much quicker due to its location next to the sea.

Buildings were cracking or already demolished. Anything made from iron was rusted and leaking orange coloured liquid which stained most walls and roofs and leaked down onto the ground before pooling into stinking puddles. It was a depressing sight but didn't bother the group as they were more occupied with the objective at hand.

They stopped for a moment, opening their rucksacks and donning plastic overalls which went over their clothes and which they hoped would give them some slight protection from the radiation or other hidden threats they might encounter. Their boots were covered with plastic bags and their hands protected by medical style gloves. The plastic seemed as if it was brand new, although it was scavenged from a hospital just after the collapse.

The streets were barren of people or other life and to Otto, who was getting nervous once again at the thought of seeing the lurking shadows, it was a relief for him when the windows of all of the buildings which still stood had nobody shadowing their door or window silhouettes.

Down the main street on which they walked they could see the rolling waves of the channel in the distance. The water was choppy and beat against the concrete flood barriers which were being battered by wave after wave of salty, frothy water. Pebbles from the beach were littered across the road tens of metres away and had become like a layer of marbles which made the group slip slightly as they cautiously made their way towards the water.

Arthur stopped, opening his box and taking out the Geiger counter which ticked slightly from the normal background radiation which was always present.

"How does it look?"said Claude.

"We're just getting background signals at the moment. Radiation which is naturally occurring and all around us. If its starts clicking rapidly then it will mean that there is another source of radiation somewhere" replied Arthur, trying to remember the small amount of information he was taught of the subject at university.

They nervously crept towards the edge of the water, always looking around to make sure they weren't being followed or watched.

The beach was covered in debris and
trash which had washed up. Plastic and
wood, fishing nets and lobster pots
seemed to cloak the beach and even
larger objects including a fishing trawler
which was overturned and had a large
hole in its side rested on the shingle. Its
hull rusting from the ever repeating
waves which lapped against it.
Arthur stood at the front of the group
and moved the small clicking counter
around in the air, getting the same read-
out. He then moved it closer to the water.
It began to click faster and faster as he
held it a few feet above.
"That's not a good sound" said Wulf, who
was still stood on the dry pebbled
section of the beach.
At the sound Otto promptly joined him in
getting away from the waves.
"Is the water contaminated Arthur?"
Claude sounded concerned, wondering if

they had all been irradiated or not.
"It is definitely higher than healthy background levels. Normal levels are below fifty counts per minute, at the moment the Geiger counter is at one-hundred and thirty counts per minute. Something has leaked into the ocean and is causing it to become slightly radioactive."

At this point Claude had retreated back onto the higher pebbles with Otto and Wulf. Arthur began making his way towards them not as concerned as the others.

"Personally I wouldn't eat any seafood from this water. You wouldn't want to take in radiation that high, unless you wanted to grow a few more arms or an extra eye" he smiled as he saw their faces contort in horror.

"We aren't in danger standing this far away are we?" said Otto

"No, we should be fine unless we drink or eat anything in that water."

He looked out over the choppy ocean, in the distance huge cargo containing ships could be seen. Static on the horizon and slightly overturned, rusting like everything else made from metal which was touched by the water. They had been left during the collapse as their crew had died from the illness or vacated to the mainland, leaving the vessels to slowly rot and sink with their cargo to the bottom of the strait which was once one of the busiest in the world.

"Those ships are also a worry, if they are leaking then that will pollute everything for hundreds of miles around. I don't think we will be having any fish and chips for a long time if that's the case." said Arthur.

The sun began to make its way towards the horizon as the day came to a close. They began their trek back northwards. Stopping at an empty house, solitary amongst the fields and forests. A fire was built for their evening meal of salted meat and vegetables. Another fire was made a few hundred metres away to burn their overalls, which they feared were contaminated with radiation.

Howls could be heard in the distance as wolves prowled the Downs looking for their next meal.

▲ ▲ ▲

The night was long and uncomfortable. With the freezing chill which blew from the southern shore made them cold to their bones and the sound of the wolves in the distance made them shiver with fear.
It began snowing lightly during the night, with the snowflakes landing on the soft earth before melting as the darkness gave way to the rising morning sun. They each took turns to keep watch during the night which broke up their sleep and left them exhausted but kept

them alive, as the wolves circled them looking for a weakness to exploit before moving off when it was found to be to dangerous for them.

Once dawn arrived they had some respite and the wolves stopped their racket up in the hills, filtering back to their hidden dens.

They had a small breakfast of dried fruit and nuts before setting off back towards the Trundle to rendezvous with the others and make it back to the Fortress. They walk in a line in order to be harder to see if anyone was further up the road and they made good progress before subtle movement was detected in the distance by Claude.

They each dived into the undergrowth when he made the hand signal to alert them. Then they waited. Watching carefully for who or what was coming towards them.

A few minutes passed and a small group of people were walking along the road speaking to each other in loud tones. They were clearly lost and were beginning to panic, turning on and blaming each other for their predicament.

The group which numbered ten walked passed the four men hiding in the undergrowth, not noticing them in the slightest. At closer inspection Claude noticed that they all looked malnourished, their clothes ragged and torn. The smell coming from their unwashed body almost made Otto gasp but he held it in, not alerting them to his presence.

Claude looked to Wulf and then the others before nodding and jumping up and onto the road, startling the group of living-skeletons.

"Halt!" he shouted.

The group stopped and stood still, many of them looked in shock.

"You are surrounded, do anything funny and you will be slain."

They stayed silent, some had their mouths hanging open in absolute fear. The other three crawled from the undergrowth and stood in a line next to Claude, their weapons at the ready. A silence fell before Wulf broke it with his gruff voice.

"Who are you and where are you all going?"

The group looked at each other before one of them, an older man with a wrinkled face, who's skin had began to sag on his skeletal body.

"We are from the East, our great leader sent us to find more land to farm in order to feed the people" he croaked, "Unfortunately according to reasons out of our control we have had a gradual shortage of food for the last few years which we believe was caused by the climate of our area."

Claude and Wulf looked at each other

surprised.

"Well wherever you are heading then I would suggest not going towards the coast unless you want to grow a few more toes. Another suggestion is that you head back the way you came immediately" Wulf, in his commanding tone, watched as the speaker of the group shrank back into himself at such a suggestion before he began to sweat.

"We can't go back, our great leader wouldn't allow us to come back empty handed. Do you have any food we could obtain, we could pay you? Please!" he began begging, taking a step forward which made Wulf move his arm into a more appropriate position for striking, his hand gripped tighter to his axe handle.

"I think you should take the suggestion he just gave you and go back the way you came old man" Claude, trying to calm the situation before blood was spilled.

The man knew that he was in a

precarious situation, believing he and his comrades were surrounded.

"Okay we will go" he said in a wispy tone.

The group of hungry skeletons began shuffling back down the road as quickly as their weak bodies could take them towards the east all the while being closely watched by the four men. They went back into the undergrowth, and waited to see if the group came back to try and surprise them but it didn't happen.

They went back on their way taking a long and more difficult route through fields and foul smelling marshland which spread out from the just before the beaches and around the small estuaries which dotted the area.

The crunching of frozen leaves under their boots became less and less as they got closer to the steep barren slopes of the ancient hilltop and once again they followed protocol and unfurled their banner once they got close enough to be seen.

They were shocked as they marched slowly towards the gate and came across a group of corpses lying on the bare ground next to the palisade wall. The old man at the front covered in blood and with an arrow sticking out of his wrinkled throat. His comrades lay about him, some face down and some face up covered with a layer of arrows like pin cushions. The crows in the woods below began making a loud racket, as their meal time had been disturbed by the three men.

They stepped over the cold, dead bodies and up to the gate which slowly opened just before they reached it.
They stepped through and were greeted by the commander of the guard, an older man with greying beard and hair named

Carnix, and some of his men.

"What happened? We saw that lot on our way back from Selsey and told them to push off back east from where they came" said Claude pointing to the pile of bodies.

"They came to the gate and were begging for food which we refused. I told them to go away but they didn't listen so they tried to climb over the walls and we peppered them with arrows for their trouble."

Claude shrugged, not feeling any sadness for the bodies outside the gateway. They were punished for their stupidity, paying with their lives.

"What are you going to do with the bodies?" he said, trying to make conversation while they waited for the last few stranglers to collect their things and join them at the front gate.

"We will leave them for the wolves, they must be getting hungry this winter. We can hear them howling every night and when we see them they look on the thin side."

Claude just nodded in agreement.

It wasn't long before the last few people were at the gate and they set off as a large caravan of people and carts, destined for the Fortress.

Chapter VI

The low covered heathland and large solitary pines of Blackdown were covered in the icy layer of frost which had been deposited during the night. In the midst of the pines stood a large, long dead remnant of an ancient oak, huge in size. It had no branches, with only the trunk and a large canker which sat at the top of the trunk and was the most likely cause of the trees eventual demise. The bark had been stripped and the white flesh underneath had been carved with figures and animals, ancient symbols and patterns and then painted to make a radiating scene in the otherwise dull and brown winter setting. Surrounding the tree were many offerings, from stones of varying sizes, small hand-made items and food.

In the surrounding area were many small huts, made from branches. Their wattled walls covered in daub, the roofs thatched and covered in a mixture of frost and snow. The smoke from the hearths spiralled out of the small hole in each of the roofs and disappeared into the sky.

Blackdown was the newest of the three settlements and was still under construction by its inhabitants who were led by Anderson. Those of the people who hadn't gone to the Jul festival at the Fortress stayed in their huts, keeping warm and spending time with their friends and family. Sentry's kept guard on the unpainted palisade, walking many miles each day around the perimeter. It was a boring job for many, with the only disturbances being the occasional curious Lynx or Wolf prowling around in the low heather.

The view over the landscape was beautiful, a sea of trees stretching to the horizon, occasionally being drowned in a cascade of fog which blanketed the countryside.

Sterinx, one of the older members of the sentry and a close and loyal friend of Anderson was doing the boring patrol as he always did in the morning.

When Anderson was away he was given the temporary command of the settlement and its day to day running. The usual number of around four-hundred inhabitants was reduced to around eighty, those who preferred not to travel or were important to the daily running of the settlement. Some of them being rather old and not accustomed to travel. Others just wanting to stay in their warm huts with their families.

The day was very much the same as the day before. With a clear blue sky after a night of clouds and light snow before the sun appeared and shone down upon the frozen landscape.

The only sounds being that of the robins and blackbirds which were numerous and loud amongst the foliage on the hilltop. In the distance rolling snow clouds could be seen to the south and from the north clear skies giving way to clouds on the horizon.

A slow rumbling was coming from the north, getting progressively louder as it got closer.

Sterinx initially believed it to be a distant storm approaching as was common in the winter months on Albion but he noticed a difference as the sound got even closer. A drumming sound which he couldn't believe.

"Heimdal come up here and listen to this!" he shouted towards one of the men who was standing guard at the gate. The man made his way up the soil banked slope with some difficulty as he carried his shield and long seax at his side which got caught on the soil more than once as he climbed the small embankment and stood next to Sterinx with his ear cupped, thinking it was a practical joke.

His faced changed with anxiety when he could hear the drumming reverberating in the distance.

"Drumming?" he murmured

"Yes, get all the men armed and tell them to get to the walls immediately. All the women, children and elderly should be ready to head south if I command"

Heimdal saluted and jogged back down the embankment and towards the barracks.

The barracks was small and stuffy with large beams of wood overhanging the sleeping quarters and games room. The roof was thatched but it was warm from the multiple hearths which burnt in the middle of the room with a red glow.

Heimdal burst into the games room where a dozen men were sat around playing cards and chess to pass the time as they rested and prepared for guard duty later in the day.

"We have a problem, everyone has to go to the wall right now!" he shouted, breathing heavily.

"Why? Wolves again?" asked one of the card players sarcastically.

"No. Their is drumming on the horizon and it is getting closer as we speak, their must be a host of people coming from the North so we need to be prepared just in case they are a threat, so get ready and get to the wall."

At this the men jumped into gear and began donning their armour and grabbing their arms from the armoury which was located at the back of the smokey building.

Heimdal made a circuit of the settlement gathering up as many men who could fight as possible, and telling the others who couldn't fight to gather themselves at the main hall in five minutes so he could speak to them.

After a few minutes had passed and he

had made his rounds collecting everyone and sending them on their way towards the walls he jogged towards the main hall. It was built much like the barracks with a thatched roof and wooden walls, however it was larger and inside it had large oaken tables which stretched from wall to wall. Around the edge stood many items which had been hand-made by the inhabitants and also some tapestry's of nature scenes and battle which were highly valued for their beauty.

The hall began to fill rapidly with the young, old, sick and infirm. The wives of many of the men who were now taking up their positions on the wall, stood with their young sons and daughters in the hall. Their was a feeling of fear as he walked into the building, people turning their heads quickly, some standing as they saw him as a sign of respect. A silence fell as he stopped in the middle of the room.

"Thank you all for coming here at such short notice. Earlier me and Sterinx were stood on the wall and could hear a drumming sound coming from the distance to the north. The garrison has been formed as a precautionary measure while we find out who the people drumming are and what their intentions may be."
Worried looks shot across the room.
"They may just pass by us but they may not. You all have to stay calm and I will let you know more as we find out." He finished trying to be as calm and composed as possible but could see how terrified the people were.

On the embankment Sterinx was trying to see into the distance using an old pair of binoculars. The drumming was getting much louder but he couldn't see anything due to the trees and plants which were clinging to the edge of the hill and blocked his view and the morning mist which drifted in and out of the trees like wisps. On the walls the men stood with theirs shields and spears waiting patiently. Even with the garrison formed they felt understrength with much less than half of the small population left to defend the settlement.

They waited, listening quietly as the drumming got nearer. A large selection of brightly multicoloured flags could be seen in the distance past the treeline, hundreds in number and It wasn't long before they could see people marching towards them, moving awkwardly through the pine forest before stopping at the base of their settlement, where the trees were cleared away. A lone man made his way from the front of the Horde and walked towards the gate.

"I am a messenger of our Lord Vesh, he demands you surrender and open your gate to his Horde and subjugate yourselves to his laws and customs. If not you will be slaughtered and the ones who survive will be enslaved."

Sterinx was shocked at such a demand. He lent over the wall and looked at the pitiful messenger who was covered in mud and looked like he hadn't bathed in many months or even years. He noticed that he looked better fed than the other people who stood behind him however.

"Tell your leader that I refuse his demands. If he wants to take this place then he will have to take it over our dead bodies." His answer made the messenger shuffle on the spot, knowing he would face the wrath of his leader due to the answer he received.
The other men stood on the wall also knew what this meant and some shifted in their armour, nervous. They knew what such a command would mean and

with such a small force it was a forlorn hope.

"As you wish" said the messenger timidly before scurrying back into the mass of people.

"Heimdal, tell the others to try and get to the Fortress and tell Cyril to prepare. Go with them if you must. We will fight to the death and try and keep them occupied for as long as possible" Heimdal nodded before going down to the hall to tell the people what they must do. He decided on the spot to stay and fight with his comrades against the menace outside the gates.

He burst in the room and began telling them what to do. Some women began to cry once they realised they wouldn't be able to see their husbands again. The old knowing a long journey might take a toll on their body and they possibly wouldn't make it. They did as they were told

though and began to collect their things and headed through the muddy road of the settlement to the southern gate.
It opened slowly and they filtered out moving quickly into the woodland behind, they feared of being surrounded although it would have been difficult for the enemy to get around the side of the wall with its steep banks of dirt topped with Palisade.

On the palisade the men readied themselves for the fight. They had the spirit of a force that knew it was going to lose but continued to fight, like a cornered animal. Stones and other masonry was being brought up to the wall to be used as projectiles against the enemy. They only had a short time to get ready for the frontal assault on there position and could see the enemy moving into position for the first assault that could happen at any moment.

Slings and bows were collected and water was being boiled.

They could see the enemy forming up beyond the tree line below them, they noticed how thin many of them looked and how ragged their clothing was. Most had no armour of any description and their weapons were crude, many being homemade.

Some drumming indicated their movements and they began to march towards the wall. Some of them carrying ladders, some were homemade from branches tied together and others were from the old world and scavenged.

"Get ready!" shouted Sterinx, grabbing a rock from the pile next to him for when the enemy was within distance.

"When they are in range fire at will!" he screamed

At this command a few of the men who had bows began flinging their arrows at the mass of bodies who were running towards the walls in an unruly manner. Each arrow led to a scream as one of the Hordes footsoldiers fell to the ground in pain. Arrow after arrow began to fly at a rapid pace. Some of them fell silently, dying instantly from being hit in the head or vital organs,

The foot-sloggers of the Horde who were hindered by those at the front began to pick up speed when they could as an instinctive but futile attempt to escape the hail of arrows flying towards them. Many putting their hands up in front of their faces, hoping it would stop one of the sharp projectiles from piercing them. A ladder carrier was hit in the neck, falling to the ground in a heap as his artery spurted blood like a fountain, he was replaced by the next individual who picked up his ladder and continued running, slipping slightly on the blood and mud that squelched below his feet.

As they moved forward the amount of

bodies of the fallen could be seen behind them. Dozens of men from the first wave lay dead or dying in the mud, screaming and crying in agony if they hadn't already perished.

Still more than two dozen men reached the wall and began putting the ladders up under constant heavy arrow fire. Sterinx threw brick after brick at the assailants and could see them trying to block the heavy objects falling towards their bodies. Crying out in agony as some of them hit their target with a bang. At least one of his thrown bricks hit an enemy footsoldier on the top of the head, knocking him unconscious and making him crumble, face first, into a heap in the mud and blood.
Heimdal was scrambling back up the slope towards the parapet with a basket of stones in his hands for his comrades, putting it down and throwing a few at the enemies below.

Some of them began climbing a ladder to the left of Sterinx, climbing quickly but fumbling due to holding their weapon while trying to scramble up towards the pointed top of the palisade. The sticky tar which covered the wall clung to their skin and clothing, irritating and burning them.

It was now that Sterinx unleashed his most brutal of tactics. Motioning for the men by the fire who were boiling a large pot of water to make their way to the ladder in question.

They lifted the heavy pot which was attached to two long wooden poles with a struggle and hobbled over to the wall. Their hands covered in mitts to protect from the scalding water and pot which swung precariously with each step. They counted to three before lifting at once and pouring the contents over the wooden wall as a hand from one of the enemy's was grabbing onto the top and ready to swing over.

The screams from the other side of the wall were horrifying to the defenders and attackers alike. The six men climbing up the ladder became like melting candles as their skin was scalded and began peeling off from the boiling liquid which covered then head to toe. Blind, they began flailing and then they fell the height from the ladder which added to their agony as they hit the ground, breaking their legs, ankles and some their necks which ended the agony instantly for those lucky few.

Sterinx looked over the wall and could see those that still held to life crawling around in the mud, he had never seen a more gruesome sight in all his life.

They crawled in the mud not even screaming now as the pain was too much. Their skin was leaving a mixture of pink and red marks on the ground as they moved, like the trail of a slug. Bone could be seen on one of the men's heads as the water had literally burnt away the flesh.

"Oh..." said Heimdal, as he vomited. The sight and smell was too much for him.

"Put them out of their misery" Sterinx shouted to one of the archers who was stood to the spot, frozen in shock at what he had just witnessed.

The other footsoldiers from the horde had began to flee back to their camp. Tripping over their comrades who were laying on the cold ground screaming or asking for help. Before disappearing back into the woodland.

The defenders could rest for a few minutes, grabbing a drink of water which was brought up to them from the well by some of the younger inhabitants who had decided to stay and fight. The rocks and other projectiles were replenished and the ladder was lifted over the palisade and thrown down behind them to stop the enemy from using it again.

The defenders knew it would only slow down their enemy. Nobody was injured and some bandages were brought from the hut they used as a makeshift hospital for when the inevitable injuries began to show.

Heimdal rushed to the back gate to check it was locked and barred as best as possible, they were locked in and flight was no longer possible. He accepted his and his comrades fate.

The enemy was mobilising again beyond the woodland and they could see a great mass of people marching towards them. At the front were those who had fled, being used as human-shields for the next wave. They were chained together and forced to march with the next row which were holding ladders and grappling hooks, hiding behind them. The bows opened fire once again and their barbed tipped arrows hit their mark with expert precision. One of the men in the human-wall was hit and fell to the ground, dragging those next to him down as well and slowed their progress towards the wall. From the back a large brute of a man stepped forward with an axe and hacked at the dead man's arm. Severing it they then went back to full pace and were at the palisade and putting up their ladders in record time.

Rocks, pebbles, bricks, boards of wood, logs and anything that could be lifted and thrown was used to full affect on the enemy out of desperation.

Some fell from the ladders and crashed onto the ground only to be replaced as soon as they fell. More and more reinforcements from the woodland began running towards the wall as the defenders were busy dealing with those who had began to climb and were close to scaling over the sharpened wooden points.

Grappling hooks were launched and

most missed their mark or were caught and thrown back over the wall. Some caught and held so had to have their rope cut. The ladders were more effective and as the besiegers began climbing they were poked at and sliced by the defenders viciously. The blood was flowing like a river as man fought man in a prehistoric struggle for survival.

Heimdal fought next to Sterinx with his Seax gripped firmly in his right hand and his shield in his left. A ladder next to him began to shuffle as the enemy climbed up it one after the other. He stood ready and as the first combatant crested the precipice he thrust with the sharp blade, catching him in the chest with a thud. The man's air left his chest as the lung was pierced and he fell back in an unconscious stupor, dislodging the blade and squirting a pint of blood across the frontline, as he fell one of his friends was dragged down with him. He was quickly replaced by the next man in line to climb the ladder.

Soon the wall was pierced and it became a mêlée of medieval proportions. Skulls split and bones were crushed. Heimdal signalled for them to fall back towards the great tree for their final stand. A fighting retreat commenced and many were slain on both sides, but it was the defenders who began to shrink while the attackers only swelled as more got over the wall.

"Run Yokels, Run!" screamed the large brute as he charged headlong at Heimdal. He thought the slight man was an easy target but miss judging the prowess of his martial skill soon regretted his decision.
Heimdal side stepped his headlong charge and pulled the Seax across his abdomen, gutting him like a fish which had just been caught on the riverbank.

His innards fell to the floor and began to be dragged along the dirt as the brute turned around to face him. Not quite sure at what had just happened as the adrenaline flowed through him.

His body began to shut down as he fell to his knees and Heimdal stepped towards him before dealing the final blow, taking his bulbous head from his shoulders in one expert swing.

They retreated and reformed at the tree as the enemy massed itself and still climbed over the wall in a human wave. The defenders were outnumbered by three to one as they faced down at the centre of the settlement. Projectiles flew and men fell as they were hit on both sides. The defenders being better armoured withstood the barrage before the rabble of Horde footsoldiers moved forward.

Sterinx slashed at them with his Seax,

dropping man after man before he was overpowered in the maelstrom of death. He was pulled to the ground and hacked to pieces by axe and knife.

One by one the defenders fell, with the tree overhanging the proceedings drank the blood which soaked through the soil and watered the dormant seeds of its fruit.

Heimdal was backed up to the tree. One of the last defenders as they still fought to the bitter end.

"See you in the next life brothers, For Victory!" he shouted to his comrades as he charged at the enemy in a rage of fury taking a few of them as he fell under the deathly blows of metal and wood. His skull split and the grey matter leaked out before his lifeless corpse was dragged into the storm of steel.

As the last man died the enemy began turning on itself, and order had to be restored with the sounds of whips cracking before they finally calmed down and began to loot.

The gate was unbarred to allow the rest of the Horde to enter and they entered with vigour. The looting was in full swing, the supply of food was quickly gathered up and taken to their leader.

He was carried in a litter by six of his personal slaves who grimaced and struggled under the weight and strain. His litter was furnished with pillows and other comforts.

"You" he said pointing at a more well armed and armoured henchman, "How many men were lost taking this god forsaken place?"
"Err... around ninety men I believe my lord", their was an air of panic in the man's voice. Not knowing if what he said could get him killed or worse.
"Ninety? Against these country-bumpkins, you should all be ashamed of

yourselves" he said before yawning. "Burn this disgusting place and cut down that ugly tree. We march at dawn", with a click of his fingers the slaves hobbled around and took him back out of the main gate and towards his vast encampment which stretched into the distance.

It didn't take his henchmen much encouragement as they looted and burnt the place, surprised at the fact their was no women or children to be found and enslave to add to their legions of chattel. The bodies of the dead, both friend and foe, were piled in one stinking heap to rot in the middle of the settlement.

The wooden structures were quickly ablaze in that orange glow and the air was filled with the sappy smell of pine and choking smoke. All of the hard work was gone in the space of a few minutes, with only the settlements wall being left untouched, its gate was destroyed to deter future reoccupation.

The huge oak at the centre was being chopped at by a large group of henchmen who revelled in the spectacle. The axes biting into the hardened wood and chipping small fragments off. Some of them tried in vain to light small fires at the bottom of the trunk but the fire would not catch. Eventually the smoke from the other buildings became to much for them and they gave up, allowing the natural monolith to live a bit longer amongst the ruins. Its carvings looking down on them and laughing at the futile attempts and cursing those who attempted it.

The Horde had destroyed their first hurdle and now prepared themselves for the final push into the heartland.

Chapter VII

After many hard days sweat and toil the defences of The Fortress were finally completed. The palisade was reinforced and weak points were found and strengthened. Stakes and other deterrents were put in front of the wall, many in a large dry moat which had been dug around the perimeter and was eight feet deep at the centre. Even further out in the woodland at the base of the Downs were more defences In the form of primitive but effective traps.

Many of them being holes dug with a spike in the centre in order to catch an unsuspecting enemy and injure them putting them out of action or in the post-collapse world lead them down a long, painful death through infection. Others were just simple holes in the ground, deep enough to break an ankle or trip an enemy, and then covered in a layer of undergrowth to keep them hidden.

Trees closer to the Fortress were cut down to the great sadness of the inhabitants. It was to stop the enemy from using them as cover or to battering rams and ramps to breech the walls. The large trunks were brought into the settlement and used for various purposes including arrow and spear shafts and on reinforcing the defences.

Nature would take its revenge on the Urbanites in many forms.

Cyril was helping finish some earthworks on the periphery of the moat with Anderson when they spotted the group walking towards them from the North.
"To arms!" he shouted and the men jumped from the moat and made their way inside at double speed.
The gate crashed closed behind them and the alarm had already made its way through the settlement and an array of

men putting on mail shirts and other pieces of armour flowed from many of the buildings. The Seax's on their hips quickly in their hands and ready to taste blood.

"Binoculars" shouted Anderson as one of his men brought the valuable item to him. Peering through he adjusted the focus and was shocked.

"Open the gate!"

"What is it?" said Cyril surprised.

"They're from Blackdown"

"Open it" chimed in Cyril and the gate began to slowly open. They walked down and helped push the gate before walking out into the open ground, rushing to meet their comrades who were trickling down from the hills.

Their faces were full of sadness as they crept down through the coppiced remnants of woodland and into the empty plain in front of the Fortress. Many shivered from the cold and were exhausted at the long trek from Blackdown, babies cried in their mothers arms and some of the elderly limped with the help of younger family members.

At the front was an elderly man, limping badly due to his bad knees and hips although still walking on his own. Anderson walked straight to him and helped prop him up.

"Bob, what are you doing here? What has happened?"

"Blackdown was attacked and we fled while Sterinx led the defence" he replied quietly.

Anderson's face changed into one of anger at what had happened to his friends and folk.

"Come inside the walls, we will give you a place to stay, food and warmth" Cyril knew Anderson's temper and knew how to calm him down. He put his arm around the old man and began to lead him through the gate and towards the large house.

▲ ▲ ▲

Hours passed and after some rest and food Bob was able to explain more on what had happened at Blackdown. He told them of the drumming and how Heimdal made them all get ready to leave while after this they fled southwards towards the Fortress as quickly as they could and that was the last time they heard or saw their comrades who were in the heat of battle.

"We must strike back at this menace before it's too late" shouted Anderson in rage, knowing many of his old friends and comrades would have died. Fighting to the death rather than being captured and dishonoured.
"Calm down and think logically" replied Cyril, which made Anderson more angry but he kept quiet and sat in the corner of

the room, mulling over his anger. His head sunken into the palms of his hands which expressed his anguish at the situation.

"They must be only a few days away and their scouts could get here at any time, Anderson is right, we must do something" Earl said, adding his opinion to the mix.

"They outnumber us but are a rabble from what I have been told by Harold and now Bob so we could meet them in the field. But that would be ridiculous at this stage." Cyril stopped, thinking.

"We will have to harass them while they camp and as they move before we finally meet them on the field in our terms. We know the terrain and the land, we have the advantage in these terms."

Earl nodded in agreement and so did Harold.

"Harold you told me that you and you're people are expert hunters and trappers?"

"Indeed we are and we're proud of it"

"Good, you will lead group to harass and slow down the enemy in anyway you can. Thirty men should suffice, fifteen from your tribe and fifteen from mine. Anderson you will lead fifteen of your men and go with Harold. You know the area better than him, and your knowledge of psychological warfare will help greatly."

Anderson lifted his head and smiled at the prospect.

"I will get the men ready, come with me Harold" he stood up and was out the room, his anger gone and replaced with excitement.

They walked through the Settlement and to where Andersons' men were housed, many of them were outside speaking with those who had just arrived from Blackdown.

The anger could be felt in the air.

"I need fifteen men for an expedition against the Horde. We will harass them as they make their way through the countryside in order to slow their advance. Harold and fifteen of his men will join us. We'll be leaving in two hours and will meet at the front gate."

They didn't say a word, a few of them nodding their approval before making their way into the barracks to decide who was going to go.

Every man in the group volunteered to get revenge for their tribes people and some were disappointed when they weren't chosen.

Harold did the same and hand-picked fifteen of his best and most loyal trackers and hunters. Wulf, Sigurd and Vendel being within the ranks. Harold's group were joyous. The prospect of travelling amongst the rural landscape filled them with happiness after being stuck in the settlement which to them felt like an age of boredom.

They said goodbye to their friends and loved ones, not knowing if this journey would be their last. Some kept mementos with them believing that it would give them protection and remind them of home.

Anderson and Harold's men kept to their own tribe to begin with, but slowly began to speak to each other as friends. They had a lot in common with their beliefs and lifestyle being similar. Banter was commonplace and they each argued who would kill the first Horde footsoldier. The anxiety was with them all the way as they exited the busy hive of the Fortress and entered into the swaying trees and shrubs of the Downs.

▲ ▲ ▲

The sunken lanes which snaked there way through the countryside made travelling difficult for the Horde, as they scrambled along the muddy paths and former roads which even in the times of civilisation were difficult to traverse in motorcars and before them horse-drawn carriages.

Carts piled high with their supplies, tents and other goods they had pilfered and pillaged as lumbered south from the cities. The column of people was nearly a mile long, with those of most importance travelling at the front, heavily armed and armoured. Their leader travelling in his litter, surrounded by armed guards. The levels of importance shrank further down the column, with those at the back being the lowest of the low in the hierarchy of the Horde. The old and infirm and slaves being prodded by unsympathetic guards as they struggled to walk at the pace of those in front of them. Many of these undesirables were used as human oxen to drag the carts. None of those from the cities liked being in the countryside, the dark sunken lane which was overhung with trees made them fearful. Birds squawked at their presence, some taking to flight but all was calm as they continued to march. They had only come across a handful of deserted houses since they left Blackdown. Villages they travelled through were engulfed by nature and they had trouble following the ivy covered and broken apart road which was scattered by rusting vehicles of all shapes and sizes. In many places the road was blocked and they had to make detours which slowed them down considerably.

They marched on and the sky began to darken from the snow clouds above, the slight flurry of snow sticking to the bare branches. On each side of the column, large slopes which were covered by deciduous trees who from their close proximity made visibility almost zero.

▲ ▲ ▲

In the undergrowth, they waited. Their faces covered in mud and their clothes of fur and camouflage hid them well. A few hundred metres down the track they had blocked the road with the remains of a large tree which was long dead and rotting. Far enough ahead to allow the food carriages and other important baggage to stop right where they wanted it. Their bows were ready and the axes and seax's were unsheathed. Anderson had shadowed the enemies for miles and decided on the perfect place to ambush them.

"Oh not again!" shouted Vesh as he saw the fallen tree blocking his path.
"Move it quickly this time"
Some men scrambled at the command, grabbing axes to begin hacking away at the debris blocking there path. Like clockwork the column began to slow down and stop at the blockage. Shouts down the column told those at the back why. The people themselves stopped and began milling around, leaning on the

carriages or sitting on the cold floor waiting to start moving again.

Harold looked at Anderson who was waiting for the perfect moment to strike, his hand in a fist. A few seconds past before his dropped his fist. The signal to strike. Harold cusped his hands to his mouth, letting out a howl that sounded eerily similar to that of a wolf. It was answered down the line and from across the track.

Anderson noticed the people in the column begin looking around in confusement, "Wolves?" one said to a comrade who shrugged.

They all jumped as Harold stood up from amongst the leaves and let an arrow fly, hitting a guard in the chest and making him fall to the ground in a cascade of blood and screams. Soon dozens of arrows were flying from both sides of the hollow and people were running to get away from the onslaught. Some scrambled under the carriages for cover. The news of the strike quickly spread up and down the column. Vesh was enraged, sending some of his many guards down to see what is going on.

After running out of arrows they charged down the slopes, with shouts of "Woden!" adding to their adrenaline fuelled rage and began swinging at those who were armed. The weakly armed and terrified guards were no match and many of them fell as the steel bit into their flesh and bone. Some of them were able to flee dropping their clubs and crude knives and swords as they ran up and down the baggage train. They had neither the will or the honour to continue the fight.

Harold began to duel one of Vesh's bodyguards who struggled to arrive at the scene of carnage with many unarmed people running in every direction blocking his path. He was a good fighter in comparison to the untrained henchmen but he fatally miss stepped and had his skull crushed with Harold's axe which left his body shaking on the floor as his life left his body, Harold didn't stop as the next Horde henchman made his way towards him.

Some of the others in the group began destroying and wrecking the goods in the wagons. Throwing food and other objects into the mud and overturning the wagons and trailers. Smashing the wheels and axles before joining back in the fight.

Anderson helped overturn one of the larger wagons, its contents spilling into the dirt with chunks of meat attracting flies almost immediately. As the Wagon fell some camp hands who hid underneath it scurried in all directions like rats fleeing a group of cats.

Harold whistled and they began to jog

back into the undergrowth in a fighting retreat before the reinforcements arrived to join the small battle, disappearing as quickly as they had arrived only a few moments before. The area was a mess and the soldiers didn't know what to do as they arrived to the scene, wondering if they should give chase or wait for another strike.

Some stayed but others gave chase, getting bogged down as they began to run up the slopes. Slipping on wet leaves and being slapped by branches. To those comrades who stayed put next to the wagons they vanished almost immediately into the undergrowth. They only heard the occasional shout and crack of branches which reverberated back to them.

Harold, Anderson and their men moved expertly through the foliage and went to the rendezvous point. Those henchmen giving chase were all quickly dealt with and no mercy was shown to them. One by one them were felled with arrows. None of the Tribesmen died in an extremely successful first engagement with the enemy, Harold happy that he got the first kill and rubbing it in Andersons face in a friendly fashion.

▲ ▲ ▲

At the column people begin to emerge and inspect the damage, cautious to the thought that they may be attacked again at any moment.
From the front of the column stormed Vesh, furious. Stepping over the dozen corpses which lay on the dirt he looked at the destroyed wagon which lay on it side in the ditch. It's precious contents spoiled.

The flies which had seemingly appeared from everywhere at once were quickly feasting on the raw meat and laying their

179

eggs, rendering the food useless. They swarmed over the area becoming a nuisance. The background noise which had been tranquil before the attack on the column was now overwhelmed with the drone of thousands of wings and the moans of the dying.

"Get some slaves to lift the wagons, and don't let that meat go to waste... the slaves can eat it once they have finished their work." Vesh smiled and so did some of his more sadistic henchmen as they readied their whips.

"I despise this disgusting muddy hellhole, When we win and destroy these insects who live in filth we will pave all of it with concrete and build huge monuments over the top. Every tree will be used to power our world. It will be like it was before." He screamed and spat at no-one in particular.

"Get a group together and find those wreckers and deal with them. If you can capture some that would be better, then we can use them for sport" he said to his leading henchman, who promptly bowed before making his way down the column and selecting individuals to join him in the pursuit.

Those at the back of the column silently expressed their gratitude at the unknown attackers, happy every time one of their captors was slain. They dared not try and escape however, their was to much risk involved.

The whips cracked and they began again on their journey through the dark woods.

▲ ▲ ▲

Many hours passed and their was no sign of the attackers. Every soul was on high alert, waiting for the next fallen tree or barrage of arrows to signal the beginning of another attack but it had yet to come, giving them a constant state of fear.

Many turned to drink and the homemade

narcotics they had to try and soothe their nerves but it only gave minor comfort to them.

As the snow turned to sleet and then rain the road changed from frozen and manageable to a thick gloop which slowed them down to a crawl. The wagons became bogged down and many had to be lifted or even abandoned in order to continue towards there goal which was still many miles in the distance.

As they turned a corner in the road they came face to face with a sight many could not bear to witness, From the branches of the trees overhanging the road swung the bodies of those who were sent to track down and annihilate the group who attacked them. Their bodies were still clothed and had chunks ripped out of them by the crows which had began to feast on their flesh. The bodies numbered a dozen. Their skin already a pale colour and rigid with rigor mortis. Most were missing their eyes as they were the most favoured delicacy of the crows who sat waiting for the column to move past so they can continue with their meal.

Even Vesh was shocked at seeing the body of his trusted henchmen swinging from the branches of the oak and chestnut trees and he began retching at the sight.

In the distance Anderson watched. His years of psychological training in the Internal Security was paying off and he smiled.

A few wolf howls added to the mix and caused the column to fly into panic once again. The guards surrounding Vesh and his litter and the food wagons.

"The phantoms are back!" could be heard from the column.

Harold and Anderson looked at each

other, being only mere feet from the column hidden under the leaves and branches.

"Phantoms?" said Harold laughing quietly.

"Quite an apt name" replied Anderson.

Chapter VIII

They finally reached a suitable camping ground without any more trouble from the "Phantoms" as they called the Guerrilla group led by Harold and Anderson. Doing as they always did the natural area where they were camped was quickly desecrated and destroyed, with trees being the main target. Soon the fires were burning and the feeling of fear still hung in the air. The pale moon lit up the landscape as the clouds cleared and the shadows danced as it moved across the sky.

In the distance the sound of an Owl and the shrill sound of Wolf howls which filled the Horde people with that primordial fight or flight fear which seeped from their ancient reptilian parts of their brains.

They camped close to the main road to have a quick get away route in case of a renewed assault and the guards were stationed behind the wagons in a defensive ring.

From the distance a group of haggled, skinny individuals made their way towards the camp. Seeing the light from the fires in the distance they saw a chance of survival after having walked so far and on their last drop of energy. Most could barely walk and dragged their gaunt bodies towards the light like a group of zombies. Their clothes in tatters and hanging loosely from their skeletal frames. Some had symbols from their former group sewn onto the breast of the thin jackets they wore, a constant reminder of the life they had come from and which they still clung to. Red Stars and hammers, which seemed oversized compared to the clothes on which they were sewn.

"STOP" sounded loudly from the carriage blocking the road on which they marched.

"One more step and we open fire, who are you?"
"We are travellers from the Collective. We have been sent to find new land to cultivate for the people, may we stay with you for the night and have food?" the skeletal man at the front of the group said weakly.

The guard on the carriage smiled psychotically, he noticed how malnourished they looked and knew they weren't the skirmishers from earlier in the day. He thought of how this could allow him to gain favour with his leader.
"Of course, follow me I will introduce you to our leader, he will be happy to meet you."
The group of stragglers were delighted and happily followed the guard into the camp which was full of rowdy people. Many of them high on various homemade drugs and concoctions,

needles scattered the ground making the walk hazardous for the group. One of those in the group began to sweat, his drug addiction long suppressed by the collapse which stopped his supply now coming back to him. He became fidgety and it began to unnerve the guard;

"Why is he acting like that for?" he said sternly, putting his hand towards the axe on his hip.

"The drugs, he is a former junkie" said a woman who stood beside him, holding his arm and acting like a handler.

"Stop him or I will do it myself."

She tried her best at the guards command, moving the man away from the edge of the trail. Once the guard was satisfied they continued towards the largest tent which sat right in the middle of the camp and had its own smaller wall of guards which protected it from all sides.

They stopped in front of the wall of armed and armoured men before a

smaller, more rat-like individual, around
five feet tall and wearing a motley
leather jacket and fur, stepped out from
between the wall.

"Daniel, what have you brought us?"
inspecting the group who stood limply,
tired of the short walk and wanting the
food they were promised.

"This group just turned up at the gate
and I thought the leader would like to
see them." He answered without looking
at his superior.

"Good job, follow me." The rat-like group
commander began to scurry towards the
huge, multicoloured tent, knocking upon
its thick, canvas door which was
immediately pulled to the side, allowing
him step in.

Daniel and the others stood waiting
outside before a shout from inside telling
them to step in and bow before Vesh.

Inside the tent vast amounts of furniture
sat along the walls, covered in expensive

jewellery as well as mirrors, vases and other rare pre-collapse items.

At the other end of the tent was a large wooden chair, raised up on a large wooden platform and made into a makeshift throne on which sat Vesh who was picking apart a chicken carcass, his fur clothes covered in grease and other food matter which had missed his mouth. Around him stood his most loyal bodyguards, with the best arms and armour in the Horde. They all wore chain mail and tactical vests, scavenged from those they had killed, including former bodyguards who were constantly challenging each other for dominance and their masters favour.

The group walked through and stood in the centre of the tent, which made them crowd together. Daniel stood at the front and bowed to his leader who didn't pay much attention and continued gnawing at his food.

"Lord, these people arrived at the gate a few minutes ago wanting shelter and food. I thought that you would like to meet them before making a decision on their fate." Daniel said while still looking towards the floor.

Some of the more attentive in the skeletal group moved nervously at the point about their fate.

"Who are they?", he burped and launched the nibbled bone over his shoulder.

"They claim to be members of a group called the collective"

"Come forward" he said sternly to the man at the front of the group. The man was caught of guard and moved forward after looking around in surprise.

"Bow", Vesh shuffled in his seat bored, he had gone through this routine a million times before.

The man bowed, standing with his hands behind his back and looking at the pieces of chicken which were littered over the floor around the throne, his stomach grumbled like thunder.

"You and your people, where are you from? How many of you are there?" Vesh asked.

"Our collective is based on the coast and we have been sent out to find new places to spread our message of unity and work. Although we have yet to come across any people willing to hear our message, we have also run out of food and hope you can help us in this aspect. In total our collectives contain around two-thousand comrades." The man answered, not taking his eyes of the flecks of cooked meat.

"I see" said Vesh pondering. Standing up and climbing down from his throne before standing in front of the man. He stood for a few moments before hitting the man square in the face, knocking him completely unconscious and making him fall backwards like a rag doll. Hitting the ground with a bang. He began to twitch almost immediately as his frail body and brain tried to figure what was going on. The group was shocked, and some turned to flee but found themselves blocked by some of Vesh's' men who had their weapons in their hands.

"Unity? No, you are my property now." Vesh said before he began laughing. One of his bodyguards came from deeper in the tent, holding chains and began shackling the weeping people before leading them outside and towards the open air quarters reserved for the lowest ranked people in the Horde.

One man who had been shackled realised his chains were loose, he could slip his hands out and escape, he thought.

They were marched into the fenced off area which had no cover from the elements and sat amongst the other slaves who looked tired and close to the end of their pitiful lives. No talking was allowed and they sat in silence, getting colder and colder as the sun began to set.

The man began looking around, the fence wasn't very tall and he could scale it although he didn't have much strength left. He could see a gap in-between the carriages which led down a slope and into the darkness of the woods. The moon was bright and it would help him see where he was going and although if he was caught he knew it would be the end but he didn't care any more.

He watched the guard, he was drinking from a large glass and was swaying more and more as the alcoholic liquid began to be digested in his stomach, not paying any attention to the slaves his job was to guard.

He slipped the chains off his hand and began creeping towards the fence, moving along the floor, stopping every few feet before moving again.

"What are you doing?" said one of his comrades quietly.

He just put his finger to his mouth as a symbol for him to stay quiet.

His comrade followed his command.
He got to the fence which was made from pre-collapse chain link, metal in composition, it would be noisy to climb he thought so he had to be quick. He watched the guard again waiting for him to take the next sip of booze before he scrambled up the fence as quickly as he could, making enough noise to wake up half of the camp.
"HEY! STOP" shouted the guard, his words slurring as he tried to get to the prisoner. He swayed and slipped falling face first into the mud as the prisoner finally got over the fence and dropped to the ground before running through the gap in the carriages and down the slope. He felt weak as he more or less rolled down the slope and into the dead undergrowth.
The mud and dead leaves under his fingers gave him a sense of relief as he made his way deeper into the woodland. It was the first time he had been alone

since the collapse occurred as he and his comrades always stayed together. Not just for safety but also to keep and eye on each other and look for anti-collective elements who were everywhere as he was told by the council.

Shouts behind him kept his adrenaline running and the minutes passed before he could no longer hear the camp behind him. He felt safe enough to stand up and dust himself off, not being able to see very far in the dimly lit woods which now surrounded him. He shivered and began walking to keep himself warm, following a well worn deer track. The moon above was blocked by branches and the darkness unnerved him.

He didn't know it but he was being stalked. He was a prey animal for a more evolved entity which lurked in the shadows. Creeping along without making a sound and getting closer with every passing second. It's form being that of a dark shadow floating a few inches above the forest floor and expert in its craft. It was hungry for the life essence that the lone, weak man possessed.

Its form flickered as it moved through the branches and the moonlight was seemingly absorbed by its vantablack, void like body.

The man noticed the movement and stopped, turning around to look as the shadow stopped. He didn't see it hidden in the darkness and continued walking. A fatal mistake.

He noticed movement again and caught a glimpse of the entity out of the corner of his eye. Turning to face it proved difficult as it blended into the dark background of the forest. The branches moving, camouflaging its human shaped outline. It could sense the man's fear which only made it more determined and hungry.

He began to run, sensing danger and the entity was close behind. Looking over his shoulder as he ran he could see the sinister being moving effortlessly towards him, getting closer, inch by inch. Its arm outstretched and the claw like appendage nearly around his slender neck.

Not paying attention he tripped over a large tree root as he ran, and falling sprawled in the dirt. He rolled and kicked out at the entity as a natural reaction, his mind in autopilot at the perceived threat. His leg went through into the abyss that was its body. He was paralysed with fear as its claw finally grabbed him and began to devour his life essence.

Filaments of light began to be absorbed into the entity from the man's body as his life force was dismantled and consumed. His body began to shrivel like a corpse which was quickly decomposing, leaving only the skin which sat over the skeletal remains like a tanned leather blanket with no discernible features and some liquids from the body which seeped out and into the soil.

The entity was satiated for the time being before it slipped back into the darkness of the forest which was like a gateway from our dimension to another, awaiting for when its next hunger would commence and once again it would quietly wait for its lonely prey to wander by.

Chapter IX

Rebecca left the sanctuary of the fortress through the front gate before the sun had risen and the moon still shone brightly above the world, leaving the land in a pearly complexion. She crept along the wooden wall without a sound before veering off through a gap in the defences and towards the hills in the distance. Over field and ditch she walked, the tracks of deer, fox and badger could be seen. The deer kept the grass of the field at a low length and during the summer months, when the heat beat down cows and sheep which abounded the area were kept in the fields before going wild again in the winter.

She enjoyed the walk in the cold morning air, following the borstal tracks up into the wooded hills. She had to duck under bare twigs and bigger branches, slipping occasionally as she gained more and more height. An old track used as a footpath before the collapse led up to the bare, chalk lined face of the main hill. It was used as a beacon many centuries before. She rested for a few moments at the base of the hill and amongst a valley which had been in use since time immemorial. She sat on the stone base of a signpost which had rotten and fallen over a few years before, she remembered when she would sit there as a young girl after many hours hiking and exploring the hills.

She continued her journey up the side of the beacon hill. The hardest part of her journey due to the steepness and weather conditions which froze the ground and made her slip more than a few times. She followed the foot holes which had been dug out of the chalk from many journeys up the hill. At the top she could see one of the two guards, who were always present on the hill. He was watching the horizon, looking for signs of movement in the North and South, he was wrapped in a tartan blanket over his armour and his face was covered by a thick scarf to keep out the wind which chilled to the bone on top of the exposed hill. She waved slightly as she kept climbing to show she wasn't a threat to the guard and he waved back before making another round of the summit.

From the top of the hill she could see miles in every direction. To the south covered in fog which wafted in from the sea, was the old port city of Portsmouth and behind it the Solent which itself was shadowed by the Isle of Wight which stood like a sentinel over the narrow strip of water. In the water were the abandoned wrecks of oil tankers and cargo ships which were listing in the water, a terrible sight and one which filled her with dread. Turning around she looked to the north, immediately below was the Fortress with its chimneys allowing smoke to drift upwards and beyond that the vast expanse of countryside going as far as the eye could see.

"How is everything?" she said through her scarfed mouth to the guard, she adjusted the heavy bag on her back now she wasn't moving. The cold got to her straight away.
"Not bad. Their has been some smoke coming from the North suggesting a camp but it is near the horizon so many miles away, from the size of the enemy's horde I would say a few day's away at the most."
"The time is getting nearer, but we must face it head on" she replied before walking towards the southern side of the hill. She passed over the concrete ruins which were left since the war, the remnants of spotlight emplacements

before following the track to a quiet location she always liked to visit. She stopped and opened her bag, placing a blanket from it on the floor and then some candles which she aligned at each corner. The light from the candles gave a warm glow in the morning light which calmed her and cleared her mind. She sat an observed as the sky got lighter from the rising sun and began asking those beings she had contact with help for the coming battle. She could sense them nearby and knew they wouldn't harm her although they were unnerving. She didn't speak aloud, but her thoughts were enough for them to make their decision to help or not. The light from the candles held them back as they didn't like the flicker, she had learnt that as a young girl when they had first visited her. It was around that time when she first knew she had psychic abilities although she was confused now, not knowing the outcome of the coming battle. She tried hard to visualise it, asking for help from the Archons but it wasn't clear enough. Her thoughts were clouded. All she knew was a large battle was going to occur between the people and the Horde. She sat for hours and it was mid-morning before she blew out the flames which flickered on the candles and collected her things and making her way back down towards the settlement and its safety. She was neutral, not knowing the outcome which would occur soon bothered her but she knew she couldn't do anything to help it. The guard waved goodbye as she made her way down the steep, barren chalk hill as the wind bit the exposed tops of her cheeks.

▲ ▲ ▲

The Fortress was a hive of activity as the gate opened, armed and armoured Thegns made their rounds while others carried food, water, arrows, stones and other objects which would be needed for the coming fight. The blacksmiths were working constantly producing arms and armour. The sound of hammer on anvil became like a background song which was quickly filtered into the subconscious.

Above the noise of the Smiths hitting their anvils was the sound of mock battles occurring on the green. Shield walls fought each other with blunted or wooden swords, getting ready for the final struggle. Archers improved their accuracy against sacks filled with straw and most were expert shots.

All the while Cyril and his Thegns stood at the edge of the green and debated tactics while watching the mock battles. Rebecca's nervousness began to dissipate when she saw the great mass of well trained and well armed soldiers who were willing to give their lives so that their people could live in peace. She wandered over to her husband and listened as they talked tactics.

She waited around for a few minutes before deciding to walk to the church and inspect the fortifications which had been built around it.

She walked from the training ground and up through the old club which was still used a social area for the inhabitants, the beer taps and liqueur optics were long dry however and replaced with homemade barrels filled with home-brew which were off-limits due to the current circumstances they found themselves in.

The Church was across the road and she opened the old ash gate which creaked eerily. The churchyard was filled with ancient Yews which covered the graves with a dark and sombre aura. The ground was damp and covered with dead, brown needles and the smell of petrichor in the air was almost overwhelming. The grave stones were worn from the elements and the names which covered them were hard to read below the moss and lichen which clung onto their cold, rough surfaces.

Closest to the church were the oldest graves which dated back to the 15th Century, and as the stones drew backwards the dates became closer and closer to the present. Large family vaults were located further into the graveyard and were in a bad shape, with stonework flaking after many centuries. The Yews in between them were thriving in comparison, growing larger with every passing year and their seedlings sprouting into large clusters of saplings which were left alone by the inhabitants of the Fortress.

During the autumn they collected the red berries and ate them although everyone knew how dangerously poisonous the trees could be and respected them for it. The graveyard was still cared for and tended to by the people, many of them had ancestors who were buried within the grounds and great reverent was given. In the five years since the collapse some of the inhabitants who wished to be buried were given plots in the empty parts of the graveyard, and instead of headstones they had saplings planted on their graves so that new life could grow from their death and would feed their descendants, in which they would reincarnate, with the fruits they produced forever afterwards.

Rebecca stopped and looked across the dark area, many thousands of years before the present she knew this area was a heathen land and it was once again, the Yews being the offspring of those original trees which festivities were celebrated under and were worshipped for their life and death giving properties. The name of Woden and Thunor, Tiw, Bældæg, Sunna, Nerthus, Sigyn and the countless others which used to wander the land and once again began to wander, amongst the trees, fields, rivers and lakes.

The church was made from ancient Sussex stone, worn and weathered and covered in a fine layer of lichen like the surrounding gravestones. On top, the large copper spire shone in the winter sunlight and was easily visible from The Downs and other surrounding hills. Watching from his nest high above and within the spire was a young Peregrine Falcon, he watched the proceeding's below and had no fear of the inhabitants, they had never bothered him unlike the others which existed many years before. Rebecca walked to the side entrance which overlooked the road which ran through the centre of the Fortress and was alive with movement as men and women did their duty for the greater good of the people. Men moved towards the walls to begin their watch, some rested outside or were exercising in their spare time and making ready for the final battle which they knew was close at hand. Underneath the most sacred of all monuments within the walls of the Fortress, the Great War memorial which stood like a silent watcher. Many of those ready for battle below had ancestors names inscribed upon the stone which bore their everlasting memory. Rebecca herself had an ancestor who's name graced the stone, although his bones were still resting in northern France where he had died over a hundred years before. Wreathes of Holly and other Winter plants stood underneath it from the earlier remembrance festival which occurred at the beginning of winter.

She opened the wooden door which had intricate iron fittings which seemed to move and interlock in a pattern of great beauty and walked into the spacious but dark room. The pews and other wooden items which once lined the inside of the church were long gone, used for firewood or tool making, while everything metal was scrapped and turned into the material for arms and armour. The large wrought iron cross which once sat at the heart of the building was the first to be melted down and turned into seax's and spearheads. The spirit which was worshipped in the building was gone, disappearing at the very start of the collapse if it ever existed at all.

Some memorials to many people who had once lived and died in the village hung on the walls, some dating from the 18th century and written in Latin while on the floor more memorials, most of which were of the clergy who had formally inhabited the building. Some recumbent effigy's from the 1500s were fixed to the wall and kept due to their great beauty being intricately decorated and painted.
Her footsteps clicked on the cold stone

and she could see her breath in the freezing building. She looked up at the stained glass and the multicoloured sunlight which flowed through it showed it was frozen on the inside. Through the centre of the old building and into a back room she brisk fully walked opening a door to a small room which was enclosed the ancient spiral staircase. She crept up it, which made it creak and unnerved her. The handrail well worn from many centuries of use and she breathed heavily when she reached the top and knocked on the panel door leading into the clock room. The wind moved the tiles on the outside and a large clanking noise resounded around the draughty rafters. The knocks echoed and the door was quickly opened by a young, bearded man. He was wrapped up with a hat, scarf, fingerless gloves and a large fur coat.

"Hello, Rebecca" he said, his teeth chattering slightly.

The open door let a draft of freezing cold air through which quickly woke Rebecca up after the long and tiresome climb.

"Hi, Bran. How is everything?"

"Cold as usual" he chuckled, "No movement in the hills from what I can see, I'm expecting your brother will be back soon. He didn't take many supplies with him on the expedition." He waved her in to the room before closing the door behind. It slammed slightly from the draft.

The room was small due to the size of the large clock workings which would have been clicking loudly but fortunately they no longer worked. A large bell in the middle stood silent surrounded by a railing which allowed a view of the church floor. Rebecca tried not to look over the edge because she began to feel dizzy at such a sight.

The opening in the slatted wooden sides of the Clock tower allowed a beautiful view of the Downs and the rest of the Fortress with the wind blowing in. She found it difficult to hear with the wind blowing past her ears and it made her eyes water and squint.

Bran had a chair set up next to the opening with a pair of binoculars, a book and some food sat on the small repurposed lamp table. Next to the chair was an antique rifle, one of the few in the settlement and in mint condition even though its age was much more than any of the inhabitants. Its telescopic sights tweaked to reach the base of the Downs, it was rarely ever used though for lack of ammunition. Next to it was his seax, its blade recently sharpened.

"We expect my brother back by tonight if nothing has happened to him" she said with a smile. "Do you need anything? A hot drink or more food, your shift is for a few more hours yet."

"I wouldn't mind some soup" he replied before sitting back down and breathing hot air into his cupped hands trying to warm them.

"I will send someone up with a bowl for you Bran, have a good shift." She departed the cold space quicker than she had arrived and the rush back down the spiral staircase made her queasy. She could feel the warmer air rushing up to meet her as she braced the bannister to go back down and out into the coldness. She looked forward longingly to the coming spring and summer. The warmth which she hoped she would be able to feel again.

Chapter X

Harold crouched in the darkness holding his bow in one hand and pulling an arrow from his quiver with the other. The arrow silently slipped through his fingers and was readied to be fired at a moments notice.

Anderson, holding his short Seax was looking down the line as the small group readied itself. Their blades were darkened with mud and their faces were covered in masks made from bark as an added psychological effect to those they were about to face. Around them the grass was long and dead, with the frozen ground crunching below their feet making the slow journey towards the camp a nervous one.

Above them the dull, warm light of the camp could be seen and the loud, obnoxious sound of its inhabitants could be heard, reverberating from the chalk walls surrounding them. The crackling fire began to increase in volume, masking the sound of their footsteps. The warmth from the fire itself was pleasant after spending a few days in the cold wilderness but they couldn't spend long with such a comfort as they had work to do.

The group were spread around the small section of camp in a crescent shape. Each man was evenly spaced from the next in a ruse to make their numbers seem bigger than they actually were.

Anderson lifted his hand and they all stopped moving at the signal. He began to move forward on his own looking for guards. Out of the darkness someone stepped, almost staggering and falling over. It was clear he was intoxicated and he began to stumble down towards Anderson, who dropped to the ground luckily not to be seen.

The man moved past him before he pounced upon him with the seax.

The man had no time to comprehend what was happening before the seax did its job and had cut the artery running up his neck and his limp body fell to the ground. Soon the warm blood was melting the frozen ground where he fell and the steam from it had risen into the air. Anderson wiped the seax on the man's body before creeping forward again towards the target. All around the fire sat over twenty people. Mostly men but also a few women who were sharing around a bottle of pre-collapse vodka. The affects of the drink was doing its job as many of them were slurring their speech or loudly dancing precariously close to the campfire.

Anderson looked at each of them, twenty-three in total he counted, he decided that he would be the first in and jump through the fire kicking it as he went to cause as much chaos as possible before the rest of his men joined the fray. With military precision he knew these enemies would be no match due to the intoxicated state they were in. The psychological effect on the rest of the camp would be tremendous.

He looked back towards Harold and put his hand up and spread it with each five digits signifying five seconds before he rushed up the hill.

It only took him a few seconds before the huge flames came into view as he leapt through the fire in one movement, kicking the ashes as he did so. The ashes flew across and hit one of the Horde henchmen burning his face and lighting the tent behind him on fire almost immediately. The man screamed as his flesh melted before Andersons seax bit into his clothes and tore the meat apart from his bones.

Harold counted down from five and at the correct time he whistled and the rest of the group charged up the hill with shouts of "Death!".

They burst into the camp which was in a

state of panic. Men and women ran in all different directions. Fleeing like rats from a sinking ship, pushing past each other to try and escape from the flames and blades. Harold let off an arrow which made its mark, hitting an enemy between the shoulder blades and sending him flying into a tent which collapsed under his weight.

The sounds of screams and yells of the group soon makes the entire Horde encampment wake up wondering what was happening.

Anderson in the spark of the moment grabbed a part of the burning tent structure which was melting from the flames consuming it and launched it further into the camp sending flames gushing everywhere as the fabric took the flames like tinder to a match, before he whistled and shouted "Back!" to his group who finished what they were doing before running down the hill and towards the forest below.

The rest of the camp began to catch from the fire with the bright orange flames jumping from the tightly packed fabric and plastic pre-collapse tents. Hundreds of those in the Horde began fleeing to the centre. Some of the more intelligent tried to throw dirt over the fire to put it out without much luck due to the difficulty of digging the frozen ground. Their stores of water were quickly used up trying to put out the inferno.

Anderson, Harold and the other men were making their way towards the main road down below the chalk and grass hills. After a mile of walking they deemed it safe enough to stop and have a rest. Taking off their masks and doing a count. No losses were counted, with sighs of great relief for such a dangerous endeavour to all those involved.

They began walking southwards with Anderson leading the small group. He could only see by moonlight and had to stop a few times in order to get his bearings before finding a rotting and rusted direction sign which told him he was going in the right direction. They were only an hours walk from the Fortress and decided to head back after, a few days of strenuous skirmishing they needed a rest and some hot food.

Even with the light of the waxing moon they kept close together as they walked, remembering the stories told of the Tiger and other predatory animals which lurked in the night and those dark entities which abounded the natural world and cared not who they hunted. They spoke and reminisced of the old days about where they came from and other topics. Harold and Andersons men saw themselves as brothers now, although their differences in living they were similar in many other things and had spilled blood all the same. Their common enemy was the Urbanite and without them both their peoples could live in peace, they all agreed.

"Don't you get fed up living in buildings all the time?" One of the younger nomads asked to one of Andersons men.

"No, we do leave our settlements occasionally you know. Especially in the summer when we shepherd in the hills and go foraging and fishing."

"Ever since the collapse I realised how controlled and unfree my life really was, only now are we free although life is tougher now. I would never go back to it."

They both nodded in agreement.

They continued walking as the moon and the stars made their way across the sky in the heavenly procession. In the distant the sound of nocturnal life, Wolves howled and the common Owls hooted as if knowing their presence. The sounds of foxes screaming and badgers rustling all added to the mystery of the night and the life which was found amongst the darkness which consumed everything during that part of the year.

They walked along the breaking tarmac of a former road which snaked its way through the wilderness. Although nothing changed in the scenery apart from the gradual decrease in altitude from the hills and into the plateau below. They cut through old fields and over rusting barbed wire fences, making detours here and there just in case they were being followed by humans or other beings be they animals or shadows.

The subtle smell of smoke drifting from the distance told them they were getting close to the Fortress and Anderson took out his flag which he unfurled and then adjusted it on a branch he cut from a tree next to the old road. The last thing they wanted after the long few nights of hardship they had experienced was to be shot down by a nervous guard when trying to get back to the Fortress. They also began to walk slower, checking in front of them for traps and other hidden things which had been left for the invaders behind them.

The track they followed was the only safe option, all around them in the under brush were foot traps of all varieties, being expertly hidden. From trees huge logs were strung up and waiting to fall at the slightest touch of a wire which was low to the ground and across the path. Just in time Anderson saw the wire which shimmered in the moonlight and told the others to be careful before stepping over it.

They finally came out of the woods and into the open with the Fortress in the distance, the lights from many small bonfires lighting the horizon with a slight glow. They still trod carefully as they walked across the field and towards the main gate. Harold walking with haste mistook his surroundings before standing on a plank of wood which was covered in nails which had been placed amongst the grass, fortunately it didn't go through his tough leather boot and no damage was done although it caused him to jump in the air with fright and shout which was nearly loud enough to wake up half of the Fortress.

They got back onto the main road and one-hundred feet away from the gate a shout was heard from the darkness above the wall.
"Halt!", "Who are you and what is your business?" said the guard in a monotone voice.
"It's Anderson"
As soon as he had spoke the gates began to open with a high pitched creaking as the huge hinges strained under the

weight.

They stepped through and were met by the guards who all saluted and stood to attention.

"Good to have you back Anderson, how was your trip?" said the leader of the guard.

"About as good as it could have been, we didn't lose anyone and did substantial damage to the enemy." He opened his bag and emptied it onto the ground with the severed little fingers of many of those enemies they had dispatched.

News had spread quickly that they had arrived and soon family members had made their way down to the gate. Cyril, Rebecca and Earl were with them and their children. And at the back was Freya who walked slowly. At her sight Anderson went over to her and embraced her as she began to weep.

"I didn't think I would see you again Eadred" she said, being the only person he allowed to call him by his first name.

"I always come back" he replied softly.

After telling Cyril the information they had found and the pain they had afflicted upon the enemy a feast was made. They knew the enemy would be closing in soon and they decided one more night of hospitality and joviality before the coming storm and struggle which faced them.

Everyone gathered at the centre of the village, around the bonfire which was lit and for many it seemed like the last time it would be ignited in celebration. Others were more positive knowing that the fires would have to be lit again during the funerals of those who would be slain during the battle but they had hope in their hearts that victory would be with them.

No alcohol was consumed and food was rationed with everyone getting a fair share and some libations were poured onto the fire for the ancestors and nature. And a small amount for the Archons who they respected deeply.

As the night got later and it began to become early morning everyone began to depart to their beds for some rest. Only a small amount stayed around the fire. Those that couldn't sleep from nervousness, talking in hushed tones to their comrades about their lives and fears for the coming days. The fire, like their thoughts, began to move downward as the flames ate away at the dried beech logs and it was soon a large bed of smouldering embers which warmed for many metres around. The frost began to lay on the roofs and the grass all around but not whence the embers still lived.

Chapter XI

With the rising of the sun in the clear winters sky the beads of frost could be seen covering every surface and the hundreds of spiders webs which hung from every corner. They all arose at the light of the sun as was natural, especially in the world which no longer had any imitation, human created lighting to confuse their circadian rhythms. Those that were still awake watched the rising sun with awe as it peaked from the horizon and slowly crawled across the pallid heavens.

A drumming in the distance could be heard and some of the survivors from Blackdown began to cry or run for cover at the sound, the memories flooding back to them.

The guards determined that the enemy was still many miles away and the sound was being carried by the wind which was blowing from that direction.

Like a well drilled army each section formed up with its leader before making their way to the village hall for breakfast. Meat, dairy and bread filled their bellies and was washed down with ale or a shot or two of strong, throat-burning liqueur which gave the timid a boost of courage. Armoured men sat at the tables with their comrades and their families and a sombre atmosphere fell upon the Fortress.

Cyril sat with his Thegns and family, Rebecca comforting the children as they were confused to everything happening around them.

With the mood sinking Cyril stood up which caught everyone's attention and over a thousand sullen faces of all ages turned towards him.

"Everyone here knows that the next few days will be one of great suffering for all of us. Some of us will die for the survival of the rest of our people knowing that they will be reborn later in their descendants to rejoin us. Many of us will get wounds and be in pain, families will suffer from losing loved ones. War and strife is something none of us wanted, all we have ever wanted is to live in peace and that is what we have had since the end of the collapse and the new world we have created in its wake but we must protect ourselves and the blood of our tribe so it can continue to live until the end of time. This Horde wants to end that, it wants to enslave us or outright eradicate us in order to control what they feel is their world and only theirs. A horde which only exists to consume, destroying anyone and anything in its path. Our kinsmen at Blackdown sacrificed themselves to slow their advance and allow their families to escape and to keep their honour, we cannot allow their sacrifice go to waste. We will avenge them." His speech was answered with silence from the crowd.

He could see men trying to keep tears from forming as they remembered those friends who had sacrificed themselves at Blackdown, the fires of hatred for the horde burning within them.

From the silence Anderson stood before shouting "For Blackdown! For our Blood and Kin!" before unsheathing his Seax. His words were echoed by those gathered and the they all raised their weapons in a rallying cry which could be heard across the hills. They knew that the fight was going to for the life or death of their people.

Breakfast was finished and the last farewells were spoken between families. Husbands and wives, fathers to their children, siblings to siblings and also between the parents and their sons who they worried they would never see again. And last of all the men spoke to their friends who were in different sections, they joked, laughed and some cried before they all departed and formed up on the green to get their orders.

Cyril embraced Rebecca who had the shining proof of tears on her cheeks before he said goodbye to his children. His Thegns did the same with their families. Anderson was most effected as he said goodbye to his wife and their unborn child, although he kept his emotions under wraps with military precision, as he was taught all those years ago.

All of the one-thousand men formed in neat sections on the green in sections of one-hundred. They all stood to attention, most holding shields and spears, with their Seax or other weapons in their scabbards and javelins held behind the shields. Their armour of mail glittered in the sunlight. Each section leader read a list with each man's name in his section with each individual answering when his name was called. No man was missing as they turned out and began to march towards the fields in front of the Fortress which was overlooked by the Downs. Behind them was the palisade of the Fortress, their was no escape and each man knew that. From the walls watched those who were brave and curious while most stayed at the village hall with Rebecca and counted the seconds, waiting for the end. Others were runners, taking food and water to the warriors, and other items like arrows, stones for slings and javelins. Others waited in the makeshift hospital which had beds ready, Mrs. Rake leading a group of young women who she had trained in basic first aid and others worked as porters which would transport the injured to the hospital.

They were all under the direct command of Rebecca.

Once the men formed up on the field that they had chosen for the battle they formed a rank three deep with some reserves and ranged troops at the back who waited with their slings and bows with their arrows stuck in the ground within easy reach. Everyone was tense as they waited for the enemy to come into view. The feeling could be felt in the air.

In the distance the drumming was getting louder and louder as the Horde got closer towards them. Nervousness could be plain to see on all the men's faces. Some were reassured as Cyril walked down the ranks, speaking to each of them. Tapping some on the shoulder and giving words of encouragement and raising their spirits. Inside he was immensely proud of his people and what they had accomplished in such a short amount of time. It saddened him that he would lose some of these great men in the grips of war and suffering but he also knew that this battle would temper their spirits and help them in the future if a threat ever made itself known again.

Stood in silence apart from the occasional murmur or cough, in the distance the rhythmic drumming and the sound of birds singing in the late morning sun.
Soon after the first signs of banners of many different colours could be seen upon the Downs, they had no symbols on them and seemed to be made from torn fabric. A vast amount of bodies scrambling amongst the trees like insects coming towards the orderly lines of infantry. Once they arrived above the treeline the movement stopped and so did the drumming which left the peaceful sounds of nature over the land.

Cyril waited. His mind going over all the events which could take place and different battle tactics he could use but he knew that the enemy had a numerical advantage and would try and use that to its fullest, his only hope was that a better trained force could defeat the mass of rabble. He knew throughout the aeons of history that it had happened many times and that the smaller force could change the tides against their larger and stronger foe.

From the distance a lone figure was making his way towards their lines. He walked carefully as he spotted the traps and other battlements which were built to slow down the enemies advance. As he got closer Cyril could see it was an older man, with grey balding hair and a greying beard which was thin and wispy on his face. His clothing was much like the rest of those in the Horde, tattered and a mixture of old world clothes which had been scavenged from the ruins, while over the top he had newer furs for warmth.

"Hold fire!" shouted Cyril.

"A messenger?" Earl whispered to him.
"I believe so, we should hear what he has to say although I don't believe it will be to our liking."
Cyril, Earl, Anderson, Harold and some Thegns walked forward from the vanguard of their men towards the lone man as he still walked slowly with his back hunched across the field towards them. They stopped and waited for him to reach them.
"Stop!" said Cyril when he decided the man was at a suitable distance.
The man did as was told and stopped, he was slightly out of breath after the long walk.
"I am a messenger from my Lord and my message from him to you will be brief. He demands you lay down your weapons and submit to our eternal leader, if you kneel to him then he will allow you to join his Horde and become vassals of the new world which he is creating. If you do not heed his advice and submit then you

and your land will be utterly devastated. Some of your people will be enslaved and the rest will be eradicated and used as ballast for the great works he has already planned. What is your answer?" For the man's weak physical structure his voice was loud and dominating, like that of a public speaker.

Cyril waited a few moments, his comrades looking at him with anticipation.

"As you can see around me, my people do not wish to submit to your leader and his cruel way of life. We know what he has done to other peoples such as my comrade Harold and his people who were forced from their land by your Lord and joined us in alliance to fight back, or my other comrade Anderson who's settlement was raped and pillaged by your Horde only days ago. We believe in life and peace and are willing to die in order to allow our people to continue to exist. In answer to your question I will not give your leader even a speck of this sacred land which we stand on, his corpse will be used to feed the soil and so will any of his followers. Tell him to come down and fight, let us settle this once and for all."

The messenger bowed before turning around and heading back towards the hills in the distance. His anxiety was hidden but he knew he could lose his head due to Cyril's answer.

"Men ready yourselves!" Cyril shouted, and at his command in each direction the shield wall began to form. The different coloured shields, painted with runes and other symbols interlocked with each other, spears poking through and ready to strike the invaders. Behind the men holding their bows and slings waited for the enemy to appear and come into range.

Cyril and his Thegns joined the wall and readied their spears and javelins. Cyril was flanked by his Bannerman who held the flowing flag of his personal standard. Along the line to the left he could see Andersons banner flapping in the wind, and to his right was Earl's.

The land went back to silence with the twinkling of armour and weapons resounding.

Up in the hills movement could be seen. Many bodies began making themselves down the chalky slopes and towards the battle lines. They were too far away to count how many were formed up in front of the battle line but it was enough to cause them concern. They seemed to creep forward like a low cloud on a foggy day and the silence was then broken as screams began to ring out. Those unlucky footsoldiers who found themselves falling into traps and being impaled or Standing on foot traps and being incapacitated. The numbers were thinned very slightly but they still marched rowdily through the no man's land.

Shouts from the enemy began to be heard, "Yokel scum!" and other slurs were thrown as they still marched forward like a wave.

As they got closer it began to come apparent that these men were not prepared for war in the slightest. They wore no armour and many had no shoes and walked barefoot through the dirt and mud, their weapons were no better being a mixture of clubs, knives and metal bars. Some had axes which they had pillaged or other pre-collapse tools from pickaxes to shovels. They had no structure to their line and no formation to follow. Their only goal was to swarm Cyril's men and overwhelm them in a human wave attack reminiscent of Flanders or the Somme during the First World War.

They were still over a hundred metres

away as Cyril shouted "Shoot!", the archers began to open up with the sound of their bowstrings slapping and a barrage of arrows flew over the shield wall. The first line of footmen took the brunt of arrows and most fell to the ground dead or injured. Screams followed shouts as they were passed by the next line who now had the look of fear in their eyes and on their faces. Still they moved forward knowing any retreat would mean certain death for them and their families.

Flight after flight of arrow flew amongst them and they quickly adapted their line from a packed mass into a more spread out one.
Cyril in a strange moment of battlefield reflection was amused at how even the most stupid of foes evolves his tactics to the situation, much like a bacteria to outside stimuli. The thought only lasted a second before he focused again.

Then they came into range of the slingers who also opened fire and began to pelt the front line with stones exacting massive casualties as the relatively small, disc shaped stones broke bones and split the skin of the unarmoured men. Leaving them crying in pain on the dirt or trying to crawl back through the rabble towards the hills.

They got quicker in pace as they were now only tens of metres from the shieldwall and the javelins from the second line were thrown with vigour hitting and disabling many more of them. The wall braced for impact as the enemy smashed themselves against it in a human wave, clubs, hammers, knives and other weapons tried to find holes in the wall unsuccessfully. Some of Cyril's vanguard began to push, and the enemy pushed back. Those at the front had nowhere to go and were pushed closer and closer to the wall of shields creating a crush of horrid proportions. The spears came over the top of the wall prodding for flesh, Seax and axe coming down on unarmoured heads and limbs and soon the ground was awash with blood, spit and other bodily fluids as men were hacked to death with mechanical efficiency. Cries of pain and the death rattle became the chorus as the shield wall marched forward a few paces, pushing back their enemy who tried to fight in desperation before many of them who were further back in the chaos began to flee as their natural instincts came forward from the deepest recesses in their brains. And once one man threw down his weapons and began to run the panic amongst the ranks of rabble became a retreat and then became a rout.

"Hold! Hold!" Cyril shouted, worried that his men with the euphoria of battle in their minds would give chase and get themselves mobbed, but his order made its way down the lines and the well trained men followed his command. They all began to move back trying not to trip over the bodies left in their wake before forming up in the shield wall in the original defensive position.

Those that had been lucky to escape were running past their fallen comrades who struggled in the traps, shrieking for help and being ignored.

▲ ▲ ▲

Within the settlement the first walking wounded began making their way towards the makeshift hospital. A few men with wounds to their legs and arms were sat down and attended to, their cuts being cleaned and dressed while they chewed on willow bark to numb the pain before those that were well enough were sent back to the front lines to continue the fight. A few others were badly hurt with concussions or wounds which needed stitching to stem the blood flow and so the beds began to be filled. The nurses worked efficiently tending to each of the men while Rebecca made her way to the area asking each of the men how the battle was going and boosting morale. The people worked together like a well oiled machine with each person knowing what job they had to do for the defence of their people.

Young people were rushing to and fro carrying arrows out of the slightly opened gate. Helping the wounded or keeping the elderly and infirm company in the village hall all the while the battle raged outside the walls. Spirits were high amongst those who waited for the end of the battle although the terror was their as well as they knew what would happen if they lost. They sang old folk songs to keep themselves busy and reminisced. Mothers cradled their babies and cuddled their other children close to them.

▲ ▲ ▲

At the battlelines Cyril was making adjustments to his tactics, speaking with his Thegns and comrades. They all agreed that they couldn't stand and defend all day because they knew eventually they would be overwhelmed and that would be the end. It was decided that Harold and his detachment of tribesmen would go into the woods and do a flanking attack when the battle reached its zenith. A dangerous manoeuvre even for a well trained, professional force but Cyril decided to take the risk and Harold was happy to commit to it as he knew they didn't have much choice. His men were more used to such tactics.

All the while they spoke the next wave of

Horde footsoldiers were forming up ready to throw themselves against the shield wall once again. They were spurred on by the sight of Harold and his detachment leaving the main group and heading of into the east in a hurry.

Vesh was gleeful at the sight,
"The battle is already won, the Nomads are fleeing!" he manically shouted, his eyes almost bursting out of their sockets as he walked back and forth at his position amongst the trees overlooking the battlefield.
Below him the next formation was about to march down the hill to their fate, at the front were those who fled, tied together with rope and chains and used as a human shield for those behind them. Vesh was disappointed at the first attack, in the past he had never had to send more than one or two waves at his enemies although he didn't care about the losses, life was cheap in his eyes and

his Horde needed to be thinned slightly. Most of those in the first wave were those who he had enslaved, the next wave was a mixture of slaves and his own men, loyal to him and ready to sacrifice themselves. His followers were easy to identify as they had better weapons and armour which were all looted from places they had raided or conquered in the past. Some even carried the weapons they had looted from Blackdown, however most carried rusted and badly maintained items which they had taken from raider groups which had been destroyed by the Horde in the past months.

The drums began beating again in a dull rhythm signalling the advance and they headed back down the perilous chalky slope towards the battlefield.
Vesh decided that the rest of the army would follow and they began to collect their items of war. Many of his more

rational lieutenants tried to stop him from doing such a dangerous change of tactics but he swatted them away and they dared not resist because they knew what would happen if they did.

▲ ▲ ▲

The sound of drums broke the small rest the men were having and they once again gripped their shields and spears with determination. From afar the mass of bodies moved towards them, the front row was chained together and unarmed. Many of the defenders were disgusted at such a dishonourable sight which confronted them but they expected no less from their enemy.

The archers opened up again and began to pepper the attackers with such ferocity that many of them looked like pin cushions after the first barrage. The human shields were the most unfortunate and as each began to drop it weighed down the rest of them and eventually they were all lying in the churned mud with arrows protruding from blood stained wounds. The battlefield itself was now haphazard under foot from so many bodies which had begun to pile up. Cyril and his forces used that to there advantage and the Horde footmen tripped and stumbled as they charged towards the line.

The Shield wall held again as they crashed towards it but these enemy combatants had more martial skill than the first wave and began to chip away at men in the wall. Sword and spear bit into flesh and men began to drop, as their limbs were hacked off or their entrails were cut out. The lucky ones were those who died instantly with wounds to the head or heart. The mêlée began to overwhelm the shield wall and Cyril noticed, he barked at the top of his voice "Break off!" which once again could be heard repeated down the line and within seconds the hand-to-hand fighting was at its peak. Men screamed as they charged into the enemy who was caught of guard as the wall broke and javelins began being thrown into their mostly unarmoured ranks.

Cyril charged into the hell storm with the rest of the vanguard, his Thegns with him as they began to fight with anyone in front.
His seax cleaved one man's arm off as he turned to run, the bone protruding from the socket and which he didn't notice as his brain swam in adrenaline. From behind one of his Thegns was clubbed and crumpled to the floor unconscious before the enemy was exterminated by a javelin thrown into his abdomen. The fight was for life and death and the enemy was beginning to crumble after being enveloped and kettled. They fought to the death as they were picked

off one by one. Spears prodding and jabbing from every area, finding their mark in the guts or lungs. Some tried to surrender but their was no mercy shown as the laws of war dictated and soon the last man was cleaved, his life force leaving his body as he slumped into the dirt. His entrails hanging out below him.

"Form up!, shield wall facing north!" Cyril shouted again. His men rushing into position at the command. Cyril jogged back to his section looking down the line he could see ten men missing. Running towards him was Anderson, his mail shirt was covered in blood and broken in places.

"Your blood?" Cyril said jokingly

"Of course not!" laughed Anderson, "How many men have you lost? Seven of mine are wounded, two dead"

"I'm missing ten. How about Earl?" Cyril replied

"I don't know, I haven't seen him"

It was a coincidence as Earl wandered towards them with a large cut down his face where he had been slashed although he didn't seem to notice it.

"We were just talking about you" said Anderson, "How many men have you lost?"

"Two dead and three wounded", he touched his face and wiped away the blood which immediately reappeared from the wound.

"I think one of them caught me" he smiled and the movement of his face let more blood run down his face.

▲ ▲ ▲

In the distance yet more men were beginning to form, the last contingent of Vesh's army which being over a thousand strong was like a large beast staring down at its prey as it tried to form up into something which could do damage to Cyril's lines.

Vesh himself was in a fit of rage at the

sight of some of his best men being killed and began blaming anyone around him for the tactical errors he had ordered. His generals tried to appease his anger with little success as he ordered them all to grab their weapons and get to the front line to lead the men. Their fear was easy to see at such a command.

"My hammer! Where is it? I want it now!" he flailed at his squire who brought him the large, modified sledgehammer and bowed to him before Vesh snatched it out of his hand.

"You!" he said pointing at one of the nervous looking lieutenants, "On your knees".

The lieutenant begun to blub at the command but did as he was told hoping his leader was joking.

Vesh moved towards him like a predator and stopped just in distance. "We will win this battle or we all die" and the hammer fell like an asteroid from the heavens and caved in the lieutenants skull leaving his head deflated and unrecognizable, the hammer became jammed and he wrestled it out leaving grey matter leaking and bubbling onto the frozen leaves. The rest of them jumped before rushing to their tents to collect their weapons and armour to join the mass of men on their final assault against the hill tribes.

Their formation was disjointed with the only tactics being the slaves and other low level serfs comprising the vanguard which would absorb most of the missiles and other objects and the more experienced and higher level men would follow in their wake to destroy their enemy. Morale was low after seeing the first two waves get destroyed to the last man by Cyril's forces. Many wondered what they were fighting for and was it worth it to die, so they tried to plan their escape once the fighting began.

The drums began again and at once they moved down the hill and towards the death zone. Vesh stood at the back surrounded by his loyal bodyguards and shouted orders while swinging his hammer around, almost happy with mania at the spectacle. A few men were picked off by traps on the way down and were left to die in agony and fear as the carrion crows circled overhead and some landed in the trees overhanging the chalky slopes of the battle battlefield.

"We should send groups in my Lord, not all at once" said one, shaking general who was on Vesh's right hand side, pleading with his master.

"No, we have tried this and it didn't work. We will overwhelm them like a wave on a beach before we sack their town and take what is ours. Are you a defeatist?" Vesh said with laughter in his mouth and a smirk on his face as he watched the general almost collapse with fear and anxiety.

"No...No my Lord" he replied as he looked down and kept walking towards the jaws of death.

▲ ▲ ▲

The mass moved towards them as the sun began to climb into the sky low due to the time of the year and bathed the battlefield in a bright golden glow which shone of their armour and blinded the enemy slightly. The enemy charged towards them many hundreds of metres away and they waited with cold anticipation as the barrage began again and the arrows flew through the air and found their mark. Cyril began walking up and down the line looking for gaps in the defence and found none before rejoining the defence turning to his men with one last rallying cry;

"Fight for your wives, Fight for your children, Fight for your parents, Fight for your ancestors but most of all Fight for your Blood and its survival!"

With a large cheer from the hundreds gathered the battle began again with renewed vigour as the great mass of bodies crashed into the shields and spears. The first row of Hordish men which was bogged down by the dead bodies strewn over the ground was hewn by spear and axe while the second row pushed its way through and began to hack at the wall with club, sword and any other weapon they had at hand. Men wrestled each other to the ground and fought like beasts in the grips of death. Some lost their weapons in the fight and resorted to beating their opponent with their bare fists, using loose helmets or other pieces of armour which were lying discarded to bash in their enemies skull or even in the most desperate situations biting their opponents neck in an act of prehistoric almost non-human will to survive.

All order had collapsed in either side and the mass battle began. Cyril with his Thegns extinguished foe after foe and left a large dent in the enemies force as they fought forward looking for Vesh. Cyril looked for Andersons standard but couldn't see it in the heat of the battle, neither could he see Earl's and so he fought on, not caring that his arms were heavy as the Seax continued to strike down wounding any enemy in its path.

In the distance, waiting amongst the stands of oak and beech Harold bided his time, the last detachments of the enemy were making their way to the battle and with their backs turned they would never know what hit them.
He gave the signal and the small group jumped from the undergrowth and began to jog. Their armour and furs weighed them down but they still jogged on powered by their faith in victory and the dose of adrenaline which their

bodies produced.

Their presence wasn't noticed until they had covered half the distance and then it was too late for the men in the back row who took the brunt of Harold and his men's devastating flanking attack.

They tried to flee, running into the back of their comrades who were busy fighting Cyril's men and disrupted the momentum of their push which in turn caused a panic to ripple through the ranks. Harold pushed on and his men made good headway pushing deeper into the enemy lines before they could put up resistance and the attack stalled. All around death could be found. On both sides men dropped and expired on the dirt as they battled on. The ground began to become sticky with blood and the dirt which was forced into the air created a cloud which blocked much if the vision for the men amongst the maelstrom at the centre of the battle.

The Hordes numerical superiority helped them survive for a longer time but their numbers began to fall as they found themselves enveloped on two fronts. Back to back in some cases as they fought in vain against the better trained Hill-Dwellers and Nomads.

Vesh and his most trusted bodyguards huddled in the centre of the quickly diminishing forces he controlled. They fought with the rest but kept themselves out of real danger, circling around with the flow of the battle. Vesh was looking around for Cyril, hoping that if he killed their leader then the battle would be over immediately but in the maelstrom nothing could be located without it disappearing only seconds later. His sledgehammer flew in a rage at anybody he suspected of being an enemy and it meant many of his own men fell at the end of his own hand.

Harold and his men fought with such

ferocity it even surprised Vesh and his most battle hardened troops who were slaughtered like lambs. A scene reminiscent of a berserker rage as they carved their way through and eventually connected with Anderson and his section on the flank. They had lost a large number of men who in the heat of the battle, remembering their friends and comrades at Blackdown had thrown themselves into the fight. Disregarding any and all safety and not in fear of what would happen after death, they died taking many of the enemy with them. Even the lightly armed slingers and archers joined the affray with vigour, daggers or any weapon they could find in hand.

Rebecca watched nervously from the wall, she couldn't see what was going on due to the great anarchy which was occurring. The battle lines now non-existent and the great sound of metal upon metal, interspersed with shouts of pain and the sound of struggle. She silently spoke hoping the Archons would hear her. She knew they were watching from the hills, keenly interested in the battle but not caring to get involved in the affairs of people. They would feed on the wounded after the battle be they from the Horde or from Cyril's side. Below in the Fortress the gates were now closed due to fear that the battle would be lost, and those who waited anxiously kept their weapons close to them for the eventual sound of the gate being breached. Hay and other flammable items were ready in all of the most important buildings, they were determined not to give the enemy any materials if they had the chance to sack their village, the fires which were kept nearby had flaming torches ready to be thrown at a moments notice within them and each was guarded by an elderly member of the tribe.

Children were calmed down and the older ones were told not to worry as they would return in the next life as they stirred anxiously with their friends, naturally not wanting to die. An air of defeat and sadness was all around and it had become much more silent which allowed the dreaded sounds of battle drift in amongst them.

Rebecca, doing as she did well, spoke to everyone when she could. Trying to soothe their fears and keep the morale up. Snacks and water was distributed and everyone was kept warm while they waited.

▲ ▲ ▲

Amongst the chaos men were dying by the dozen as the weapons crashed down upon limbs and skulls. Cyril and his forces fighting desperately made their way closer and closer to the centre of the enemy force and could see the multicoloured, flapping banners of Vesh and his personal bodyguard only mere feet away.

It was at this time that Vesh, in his agonizing rage decided to try and break out. He led his bodyguard which numbered some hundred individuals and they charged towards Cyril entourage knocking their own men out of the way in the charge. The battle once again became and inferno as the two more evenly matched foes fought to the death.

And as by fate Cyril saw the brute swinging his hammer which connected with the shield of one of his men, sending it splintering and flying in all directions before he finished the poor soul underneath it. Staving the man's chest in with one savage blow. The disgusting crunch of bones and metal adding to the din of the battle.

He began to make his way towards Vesh, killing a member of his bodyguard who blocked the path in the process with a slash to his exposed neck and causing a cascade of blood and spit to begin raining. At the sight some of his Thegns followed and began fighting the others, keeping them busy while Cyril charged towards Vesh with his shield raised and his Seax ready.

Vesh turned to face him and like two predators they began circling around each other.
Each looking for weaknesses to exploit.
"Finally, I have been waiting for you" said Vesh, with a glaze of psychosis covering his face.
Cyril stayed quiet and watched every movement his opponent made. Trying to work out which cause of action he was going to take with precision. Vesh was taller and weighed more than Cyril and he knew he wouldn't win in a battle of

strength but only with skill would he be able to win the duel to the death.

As he expected Vesh charged towards him and flailed the hammer around. Cyril jumped out of the way with the hammer narrowly missing his skull as it crashed into the dirt with a dull thud.

Cyril still circled patiently as Vesh turned towards him, still smiling before lunging once again.

The hammer swung and connected with his shield, creating a large crack down the painted wood and jolted his arm with the vibration. It knocked him off balance and he fell onto his back, his mail taking most of the impact. He laid flat staring upwards at the blue and grey sky with the brute towering over him, a malevolent smile on his evil looking face. It was the second blow which was about to rain down upon him when Cyril saw his chance and thrust the Seax upwards in his enemies direction. The sharpened point missed its target and instead caught Vesh in the side of the chest and made a large pool of red well up in his armour. A scream of anger followed as he looked down through clouded sight at the wound, all the while Cyril moved again, getting up from the dirt to face his hated enemy once again.

He threw his shield, as it was starting to fall apart from the crack, with fury and it hit Vesh square in the jaw fracturing it in the process and knocked him sideways and off balance.

It was now Cyril's time to go on the offensive and he did zealously moving swiftly with the Seax swinging it left and right to confuse his opponent. Like a dance he moved around Vesh, his vision focused and his breath controlled waiting for the time to strike, like a coiled snake.

He lunged forward and it began. The first hit connected with his enemy's right arm, cutting deep down into the bone and made him drop the hammer as his

ligaments and muscle was severed.
Within a second the next blow came as
slashed at his neck but it was blocked as
Vesh put up his left hand and grabbed
the Seax.
His hand began oozing blood from a deep
wound and he sounded like a banshee as
he shrieked and ran head first at Cyril
who dodged him like a matador with a
bull and thrust the Seax at his body.
He felt it pierce the rusted mail and flesh
and stopped Vesh in his path. His body
going into shock as he fell to one knee.
The blood spurted out of his body like a
fountain as Cyril twisted and pulled his
weapon with some struggle getting
caught on bone as it vacated his body.
It ground down on bone and ligament
and as it came loose with the blade being
chipped and damaged.
He swung again and the blade found its
final mark. Severing Vesh's head from his
body and with such kinetic energy
launched it a few metres into the

distance. It landed in the dirt with his dead eyes staring outwards and his tongue outstretched and limp, hung out of his mouth.

Cyril stood for a moment catching his breath, hoping that he had just ended the enemies leader but not sure. Around him the battle raged and he didn't see one of Vesh's bodyguards, who was enraged at his leaders death, running towards him axe in the air. At the last moment Cyril saw him in his peripheral and turned to block the axe coming down towards his skull. He felt the crunch as it hit his helmet, bouncing of the metal and catching his face close to his left eye and leaving a large bloody gash. He still kept his composure in the moment and his sword swung back and killed the bodyguard with great efficiency as it caught the man's unarmoured abdomen and cut deep into the space between his heart and lungs.

The battle lines stayed parallel but Cyril's men had begun to push the remnants of the Horde army backwards into the hands of Harold and his detachment.

The news spread quickly through the Horde ranks that the leader was dead. The will to fight soon began to evaporate and some tried to escape, while others kept fighting desperately hoping for some kind of miracle would occur to save them. Many dropped their weapons and tried to surrender but no quarter was given by Cyril's forces, weary of how deceitful the enemy were and remembering what happened at Blackdown. Their forces quickly collapsed and being kettled they were picked off one by one before every single person was dead in the centre. A pile of bodies stacked over a metre high was left as Cyril and Harold saw each other across the battlefield. The shouts and groans of the injured and dying were heard all around and Cyril's men began helping their comrades, dragging them or picking them up and taking them towards the gates of The Fortress which began to open and out of which ran Rebecca and the others who quickly began tending to the wounded. Their was no celebration to the victory of the battle, most of those still living were to busy tending to their comrades. The feelings of anger and hatred of the enemy was still running strong within them but began to dissipate.

Rebecca ran and shouted for Cyril before seeing him. Running she embraced him. With tears running down her face she noticed the cut down his face and took off his helmet to look at it closer.
"You need to have that stitched Cyril" she said with a croak in her throat.
"I will, I need to see how my men are before I go and see Mrs. Rake"

Harold appeared with his arm hanging limp and covered in blood. He bowed politely to Rebecca, a big smile shone across his face.

"Good to see you all just about survived" he said.

"And the same for you Harold" Cyril replied, "Did you hurt your arm?"

"Yeah one of those scumbags caught me with his club. I think it's broken but I'm no doctor."

Anderson appeared with some of his Thegns behind him, his armour in tatters and without his shield.

"How many men did you lose" said Anderson as Harold began to walk away.

"About twenty I would say, I am going to get this seen to if you don't mind, farewell" he replied with another bow before making his way towards the gate. His furs shone red in the sun as they were caked in so much dried blood and other particles of human flesh.

The bodies on the battlefield began to be sorted through with the enemy carcasses being thrown on the pile which had been created during the final act while those of Cyril's tribe were lined up below the wall in a neat row on the floor. Their shields and what was believed to be their weapons placed upon them. Their pale faces made it a sombre sight. Some of them, so disfigured from their injuries had their faces covered in fur or mail recovered from the battle so that their families didn't have to see such horrific wounds.

Three-hundred men were lined below the dark wooden palisade and it was known the number would creep up as those who were severely injured succumbed to their wounds over the coming days from untreatable infections or blood loss. When the families of the deceased were told the sad news the sounds of battle which had since faded were now replaced with the sounds of wailing sadness.

Even in the coldness of the winter day a swarm of flies began to buzz around the pile of corpses which were left in the centre of the battlefield and the crows which had waited patiently began their feast. The destroyers of nature being subsumed by some of natures most intelligent creations. Their feast not ending until the sun finally began to set many hours later.

Chapter XII

A day had passed since the great battle, those who fought rested and recuperated with their families and friends, grateful for being alive and also sad as everyone had lost friends and family in the fighting. Everyone was still ready for another attack from the remnants of their enemies who after the battle had filtered back into the countryside, but after such a desperate struggle Cyril's people felt as if a great weight had been lifted from them.

Cyril sat in his study and read from the tomes in front of him, subjects on ancient folklore and history of the area and also geographical texts which told of rock formations and their locations. He thought that the battle site needed a memorial to those who had fallen, much like the war memorial which they all held so dearly and which reminded them of their ancestors who fought in the great war over a century before. It would take many months to cut and move a great stone over such a distance but it would last forever and be a reminder for the people into eternity. Across from him sat his oldest son who was reading one of his old Tabletop Role-Playing manuals consuming everything within it with youthful dynamism reminded him what they had just fought for, the future of their tribe rested in the young, it was only with them that the world would be made anew.

Outside the sun was setting and the familiar half-light began to settle over the land, he stood and looked out the window with a tinge of pain shooting through the new stitches which obscured half his face. He could see his slight reflection in the glass and didn't seem to recognise himself.
He worried that it would be a permanent

disfigurement but Mrs. Rake assured him it would heal nicely and that gave him some solace. He never imagined that this would be his life now. He always thought he would die alone at an old age, having worked many boring office jobs and accruing a large amount of wealth which he wouldn't have enough time to spend. He had found his calling. He would never change it as even the thought of his former life gave him a sick feeling in his stomach.

He put away the books and grabbed his fur coat. The time was near.
"Come on son, go and get your things" he said tapping Lyndon on the shoulder before putting the book back in the shelf and following him out of the room. Rebecca had already left he noticed, the fire was still lit and burned slowly and warmly, giving of a homely glow.
They left the house and walked towards the open gate which in the distance could

be seen with people loitering around it speaking to one another. They walked past some who were just leaving their houses and greeted each other in that friendly, rural way before they reached the gate and the others who waited patiently for the sun to go down fully and for darkness to make its way across the land.

Lyndon ran to Rebecca, telling her of the book he had tried to read and she ruffled his hair as she carried Elfin in a sling, while Renfred and Rose stood next to her, under her watchful eyes. Anderson and Earl stood with their families before making their way over to Cyril and his family. Everyone was there, apart from those who were incapacitated and injured and the nurses looking after them. Everyone began walking solemnly towards the gate and in front of them stood the towering pile of wood and other flammable materials that was situated far enough way to not cause any danger to the settlement.

They walked in complete silence, only the wind could be heard and the final chorus of the birds before they nested for the night. The sun crept slowly below the Downs, its last rays leaving a canvas over the battlefield before flickering one last time before disappearing and leaving the landscape in darkness.
Amongst the wood were the bodies of those who had fallen valiantly in the battle. Dressed in their armour and with their weapons they lay next to one another in the huge structure. Harold held a flaming torch in his good hand while his other was plastered and in a sling across his trunk, he handed it to Cyril before patting him on the back sincerely and stepped back standing next to the others.

Cyril stepped forward and stopped, with the burning feeling of a thousand eyes on him. The journey to the pyre felt like miles as his feet crunched the frost covered ground while the wind beat against his cheeks and made him squint. Reaching the pyre he stopped and thought for a few moments of all the men laying in front of him. Many of them being close friends who only a week before were full of life, happiness and looking towards the future. It filled him with great sadness as he touched the hay and other tinder which quickly sparked into flame and let off so much heat he had to stand back.

The dusk was filled with light as the pyre quickly caught with flame and began to burn brightly and the crowd which numbered more than a thousand stepped back from the warmness which radiated from it. Some of those gathered began to cry, others toasted to the dead with mugs of beer while most just stood silently reflecting. The fire crackled and the sparks flew up into the sky as the wood burned and shifted, collapsing in on itself.

Some time passed as they all remembered those that had passed and who now gave light to the darkness. Cyril believed it was time and turned around walking back into the settlement and to the centre of the village to begin the feast in celebration of the victory. He was followed by the others, with most joining them as they made the short journey while some stayed put reminiscing by the warmth of the funeral pyre and to say their final respects to former friends and family.

▲ ▲ ▲

The feast was large and everyone sat with their families and friends while the food and drink was distributed to everyone equally. A sombreness was in the air and the jolliness of the past festivals was nowhere to be found. Mellow voices chatted and some left early, going back to their warm dwellings with full bellies and a sense of closing.

Harold ate with his people before making his way over to Cyril's table and was given a seat next to him. Cyril shook hands with him before speaking; "Harold, you have been a great friend and ally during this struggle we have just concluded and I don't forget what I promised to you when our people first met officially. From now until the end of time you and your people have unrestricted access to our lands for hunting, grazing, fishing and living and if any of your people wish to live with us then they are welcome" Cyril finished his pledge and shook Harold's hand again before they made a toast.

"And if any of you house dwellers want to then you are welcome to live with us" replied Harold with a beaming smile and a laugh before he took a large sip of ale.

▲ ▲ ▲

The days and weeks which followed the battle were a time of rebuilding for the people of Cyril's tribe. The battlefield was cleared and the bodies of the enemy were collected and transported a short distance to a bogland in which their bodies were thrown without rites. Their corpses would feed the bog and they would never be able to reincarnate or so the people believed.

The ashes of the funeral pyre were scattered around the area, some of them being scattered in the rivers and streams and being allowed to enter back into nature. The saplings, and other young plants appreciating the nutrients found in the ash as they still hid beneath the cold ground waiting for the warming days of spring to awaken them. The families of those who had perished in the battle taking some of the ash themselves as a memento of their dead kin.

A suitable stone of Sarsen was found in the surrounding areas which was dragged on wooden rollers painstakingly to the battle site and raised as a memorial. It stood like a sentinel being around four metres tall, with a further few metres of the large stone resting under the ground. On the flat face was carved 'To remember those who fell defending our kin and tribe against the horde, New Years Eve, Fifth Year after the collapse'. It was after it was raised when it became a form of ritual to leave gifts and offerings underneath the stone on the date of the battle. Weddings, funerals and other important events were held near to it as if the people wanted those who were departed to be included in the ceremonies.

They knew it would last until the end of time, long after the planet became uninhabitable.

Anderson and his people left for Blackdown, taking a few new people with them who wished to help rebuild the settlement after its destruction by the horde. On there way they found a horrifying sight. Those stragglers of the Horde who had departed from the area after the battle had fled northward and had been picked off one by one. Lone bodies were found in any dark areas next to the road. Skeletons with a thin skin left over them as if the bodies had been sucked dry of any living matter.
 The Entities which lurked in the shadows had feasted well and kept themselves hidden for the time when they next had to feed.
The column went northward itself but kept to the road carefully and moved quickly while trying to avert their gaze

from the dozens upon dozens of remains which littered every mile of the journey. The entities had no mercy and many of the victims were the weak, old and young which caused many of the people in the column distress. They had fear as they looked into the vast sea of trees and the moving shadows which flickered amongst the branches knowing that a much stronger but dormant force was living amongst them.

It took most of the day for Anderson and his people to make it back to their once thriving settlement situated on the towering mass of Blackdown. From a mile away they could smell smoke in the air and began to notice the destruction which had been caused by the Horde as it had made its way through the area. All around them trees had been cleared, only the slightly raised stumps from which once stood mighty oaks and pines remained. Some were cut and left on their sides to die as an act of hatred by the urbanites while others were set on fire and the charred remains still stood but were likely to topple at any moment.

Anderson began to feel a great anger forming inside him, but he kept silent and determined for his people. He knew that the trees would regrow, and they would regrow even stronger than before so that his descendants would be able to sit under them in the shade they would create.

The landscape was desolate as they began to climb upwards towards the summit of the hill. The ground crunched beneath their feet and the smell of burnt matter was all around. Some small patches of heather survived and was shining in the sunlight. The heath land which once abounded itself over the area was devastated and an air of depression fell over the group which continued to walk without stopping.

It took them a while to wind their way through the formerly large and encompassing evergreen glades which were now barren and a lot more spacious, before the wooden palisade wall of the settlement came into view. Even from distance those at the front of the column could see the gates smashed and hanging from their hinges the left hand gate was rocking slightly from the breeze while the right hand one was lying down in the dirt. The wood of which they were made from was blackened from smoke and flame although it hadn't burnt completely due to the large size. They got closer and a more gruesome sight came into view.

Decomposing corpses were hanging from the palisade and others were propped up against the wall itself. Their faces were decomposed thoroughly making any identification impossible, but from their dress Anderson knew they were some of the inhabitants of Blackdown. Some of his old friends.

His Rage was boiling to the surface as he drew his sword and walked through the open gate, hoping he would come across any stragglers of the horde who might be hiding in the ruins.

The entrance gave way to the open, desolate space which only months before was a thriving new living space with produce being grown in the gardens and children running around having fun in the summer sunshine.

All that was left was the foundations of the buildings which once stood, the rest being burnt to ash and cinders. All that stood was the huge Oak at the centre. Its trunk was darkened from fire and it had dozens of axe marks cut deep into its surface but still it stood, towering above everything around. Beneath was piled the bodies of the courageous and honourable defenders who gave their lives to allow the others to escape. Their bodies had been left in one huge pile after the horde had looted their weapons, armour and other belongings. The smell was overbearing for those not used to it and many began retching.

"Go back and tell the people to stop. I don't want the children seeing this." Anderson said turning to his Thegns. They did as he said and ran back to the gate.
He walked alongside the pile with a tear in his eye. All of those lifeless bodies in front of him were friends and brothers. The smell of rot and death no longer bothered him. He crouched down and began to weep with his hands holding his face. Guilt washed over him. It was he who left them after all to attend the festivities at the Fortress. Nothing could be changed now though he thought as he wiped the tears from his face, the dead

had been avenged with the destruction of the Horde.

It was during the evening when Anderson lit the pyre and allowed all those that had not been at rest to finally join their ancestors in the world beyond the living. He hoped that they would one day be back and join their descendants to live in the New World they now occupied.

Epilogue

From the foothills of the rolling Downs the tiger prowled, keeping low to the ground and sniffing cautiously. It could smell blood in the distance and the dreaded smoke drifting over the wind while its ears were filled with the sounds of human screams and shouts, steel upon steel and the dull thud of bodies falling to the hard ground. It didn't bother him though, although it peeked his curiosity slightly. He knew to keep a distance as humans are the most dangerous animal in the world and would kill him on sight.

He kept on slowly making his way through the under brush and got the scent of a deer blowing down-wind. This peeked his interest and his natural instincts and his small amount of attention directed to the fighting humans was gone in an instance.
And like a shadow it made its way back

towards the great stand of trees after his next meal.

The forest became a sea of silence. Reverting back to how it was, and has been for millions of years. The soft, cold wind moved the branches and trees while the soil and other elements which made up the area was in equilibrium.

Appendix

After the collapse many things changed for those that were still alive, and surviving amongst the ruins of the former world. Of course their surroundings changed. Nature began to colonise the urban sprawl which had spread over the landscape over the few hundreds years preceding the collapse. Concrete, asphalt, brickwork and other man-made materials began to quickly disintegrate once the elements had a chance to work on them without human interference and upkeep. If the elements weren't enough for the former urbanism, the roots of plants, saplings and trees finished the job. The hardiness of natural things had always been the bane of the urban planner and with the temperate, damp climate of the British Isles this withering of the former world was sped up at an ever increasing rate. Like the structures built by the Ancient Greeks and Egyptians, those built by the modern man were lost to time and the larger buildings were looked at with a strange awe but were forgotten as the more important parts of daily life flittered into the mind (such as surviving).

Cyril and his tribe had decided to get rid of these pre-collapse thoughts and feelings. They started anew, building their own structures of repurposing those that were in good enough condition. They respected architecture of the older sort which is easy to find in the villages and hamlets dotted between the chalky slopes of the Downs, while demolishing those that were in a bad state of disrepair and using the materials to shore up the ones they inhabited. Everything that could be, was reused and recycled.

Their way of dressing reverted back to that of the Iron Age or even older as their modern clothes which were made of synthetic materials began to fall apart. They were replaced by those made of wool or fur and which were produced by the people themselves. Leather was still used and they taught themselves how to create armour from it and metal. These ancient skills which had been completely lost during the modern age of machines and factories were learnt again. Adaptation was one of the greatest tools in their arsenal.

Language was another tool which was changing. And not just for them. The few people who survived the collapse, and who Cyril and his tribe estimated to be around one-hundred thousand individuals on the British Isles at most, had all gone into the new world with the same English language and a small number who knew foreign languages. It was beginning to evolve as groups were separated by miles upon miles of empty wilderness and so could develop their own unique dialects.

Certain new words came into use. The term 'new' being a misnomer as these words were actually ancient in origin. Cyril's tribe use a variety of ancient terms.

'Thegn' for example, is a term which was first used in Anglo-Saxon England. It means 'Nobleman' or 'Retainer'. The latter referring to a kings retainers or bodyguards.

Another example being 'Seax'. This term refers to the unique sword which became common in the tribe and was based on the Anglo-Saxon blade of the same name. It was from this type of sword/knife that the Saxons got their name. The term Seax is pronounced 'Sax'.

The laws and customs of Cyril's tribe are very much similar to those of their ancestors. With 'Holmgang' being used to settle disputes between men and women if no other way can be found. Holmgang is a type of dual in which the disputers fight each other in a ring (usually marked out by stones). They can fight with bare hands which is reminiscent of wrestling, or the more common version which is fought with seax and shield. To begin with the person who believes they have been wronged issues a holmgang to those who wronged them. The defendant has a week to respond to the holmgang. If they do not respond then the issuer of the holmgang is deemed to be just in their accusations. If the defendant answers the call to the holmgang but then doesn't turn up at the allotted time and date then they are outlawed from the tribe (which for most is a death sentence as they cannot hope to survive alone in the entity infested wilderness). Once the holmgang begins it is never a fight to the death, and seriously injuring your opponent on purpose is forbidden. Instead it is a fight until one of the combatants draws blood on his opponent or pushes him out of the circle/ring. Most holmgang are fought over personal insults to honour, and also family disputes. Those who lose are never mocked as fighting in the holmgang is seen as an honourable act to begin with and takes courage to begin with.

Another common term used by Cyril's tribe is the 'Folkmoot' usually shortened to 'moot', or more rarely 'Witenagemot'. These are a meeting between the leadership and Thegns of the tribe in which they debate a course of action for important matters.

Cyril's tribe which inhabits the Fortress, Blackdown and the Trundle is comprised of individuals from which the vast majority are indigenous to the area of Sussex and its bordering areas of Surrey and Hampshire. Their language and dialect reflects this fact as they use words and phrases which wouldn't be intelligible to anyone who hadn't lived or been raised in the area or close to the area.

Words such as 'Druv' (meaning 'driven'), 'Twitten' (A narrow path or passage between two walls or hedges) and a multitude of words which can be used to describe mud. Before the collapse the dialect was very quickly being extinguished as most people adopted more mundane forms of speech and dialect which in a majority of cases filtered from the large urban areas and seeped into the rural hinterlands like a plague. Once this stopped however, the old ways of speaking reappeared as quickly as they left in the decades preceding.

The spoken and written language was very important to the people and they put great value on books and other written material. The young were taught how to read and write from a very early age as well as being taught the other important tasks of the new world (such as hunting, foraging, fishing, carpentry, swordsmanship, how to use instruments etc.)

Another change which had occurred was that of the climate. It was noted that the winters and summers were much colder than before the collapse and thinking logically the people believed it was due to the almost instant end to all use of fossil fuels and other climate damaging processes which were used so frequently and at such an extent as to render the planet almost uninhabitable after only two centuries of mass industrialisation. The planet in effect had gone back to how it was before the industrial revolution but after only five years the vast amount of pollution created by civilisation as a whole still made itself known. Through the general litter which pocked the countryside and would for thousands of years into the future (due to the non-biodegradable use of certain materials, plastic for example) and also the more disastrous effects of oil spills, nuclear meltdowns and chemicals which leached from factories all across the world once the great collapse reached its final crescendo.

You also have those groups and individuals who still wanted the lives they once lived in luxury before the collapse occurred. Those who missed the 'golden cage' and all that came with it. Be it designer clothes or flashy cars and appliances. Some groups took their anger out on nature and tried to fight back against the flowing mass of biology which washed over the human made tumours. They always failed however. No matter how many forests you burn, or chop down or try to eradicate nature always comes back even stronger than before. Feasting on the charcoal of former forests and the decaying matter which adds more nitrogen into the soil. Turning masonry into dust which itself disappears into the dirt forever.

Nature always wins.

Wealdenperspective.wordpress.com

Printed in Great Britain
by Amazon